# Roadkill

# Roadkill

### AMIL

Translated from the Korean by
Archana Madhavan

**HARVILL**

1 3 5 7 9 10 8 6 4 2

Harvill, an imprint of Vintage, is part of the
Penguin Random House group of companies

Vintage, Penguin Random House UK, One Embassy Gardens,
8 Viaduct Gardens, London SW11 7BW

penguin.co.uk/vintage
global.penguinrandomhouse.com

Penguin
Random House
UK

First published by Harvill in 2025
First published in South Korea as 로드킬 in 2021 by Viche,
an imprint of Gimm-Young Publishers, Inc.

Copyright © Amil 2021
English language copyright © Archana Madhavan 2025

The moral right of the author has been asserted

This book is published with the support of the
Literature Translation Institute of Korea (LTI Korea)

Typeset in 11.6/15.8pt Calluna by Jouve (UK), Milton Keynes
Printed and bound in Great Britain by Clays Ltd, Elcograf S.p.A.

The authorised representative in the EEA is Penguin Random House Ireland,
Morrison Chambers, 32 Nassau Street, Dublin D02 YH68

A CIP catalogue record for this book is available from the British Library

ISBN 9781787304857

# Roadkill

# Contents

# Roadkill

Her name was Yeoreum. *Summer.* I always wondered what Yeoreum's mother had been thinking when she gave her a name like that. She must have been quite the sentimental person. Or perhaps she wanted to jinx her daughter's life. Otherwise she would never have named her after a season that no longer exists.

Of course, if *summer* simply means a stretch of time when the weather is hot, then technically summer still exists. Nowadays, every season is summer. Some regions are more humid than others, some are hotter than others; apart from those differences, they are all the same in that they are warm, all the time. The place where we lived was no different. Where we lived, it was windy for half the year and still for half the year, with frequent bouts of rain all year long. So, we referred to one half of the year as the season of wind and the other half as the season of calm. But a season by the name of summer had disappeared from earth.

However, it was impossible to know if that was reality. We had no way of verifying whether the things we learned were in fact the truth. We could only imagine – vaguely, of course – the kinds of people our mothers were. The only legacy they had left us were our distinct physical traits which made us resemble them, and the names that we were told they'd given us. We did not know their contact information or their addresses. We did not even know if they were alive or dead.

We had no other option, so we loved our mothers, or hated them, for no particular reason. We had no other option, so we accepted our names whether we liked them or not. Yeoreum was the type to love her mother. She imagined her mother to be a beautiful person. She imagined her mother living someplace in the world where a lovely season by the name of summer existed. Of course, she liked her name as well. To Yeoreum, her name was a kind of token that would someday allow her to go to where her mother lived. Day after day, she appeared to subsist on that belief.

Yeoreum believed that the animals that had once existed when summer was a season still remained on earth. From four-footed beasts like rats, dogs, cats, raccoons, squirrels, rabbits, roe deer and water deer to birds like sparrows, pigeons, pheasants, magpies and crows. Countless times, Yeoreum scoured the illustrated guide to extinct animals given to us by the scientists, ecology papers and other materials, and roamed all over the mountain, searching for traces of those animals. Proudly, she pointed out bone fragments and droppings, animal tracks, feathers – things that seemed utterly meaningless to me – and claimed they were evidence left behind by those animals. Saying that, only a few years ago, a pigeon had landed in the treetops over here and flown off; or that, until very recently, a rabbit had been living in a burrow in that nearby hill; or even that the water deer were still alive and hiding 'somewhere' on this mountain. That's how it always was with her. Yeoreum had learned about nature through her own self-study, but it wasn't a proper education. She could never specify concrete numbers, or a time or place. It was always 'somewhere' or 'someday'.

I often challenged her vague claims. So where do these water deer live? So when will you be able to go to this place where summer exists? How can you be certain that your mother is a good person? You have no grounds to believe that, everything you're claiming is just speculation, it's just fantasy, why do you hold on to such unrealistic hope? Like that, I used to argue with her.

I was a pessimist. If what we were able to see, know and experience was being restricted, and what we were able to have was belief alone, then I thought it better to be pessimistic in my belief. Because that was safe. Because, if I was full of suspicion, then I would be less disappointed. Yeoreum could not comprehend this side of me. Whenever I pressed her, she would begin by answering in her characteristic sweet, sincere tone, then snap her mouth shut and avert her gaze, and finally burst into tears. 'You're so cruel.' 'Why are you doing this to me?' 'Why do you hate me so much?'

And then I would reply in my characteristic sharp manner, 'I don't hate you. I'm only pointing out the facts. Don't get so emotional.' And then eventually conclude with, 'I can't have a conversation with you at all', after which we would spend the rest of the day sulking and not talking to each other.

Looking back on it now, I think I did hate Yeoreum a little. Specifically, her hopeless optimism. Her ability to have such an unshakeable and genuine hope toward the world. Because I could not be like her. Because when I saw her, I came to hate myself.

The government calls us a minority race. To put it precisely, we are designated a 'Class I Protected Minority Race', which means our race is to be protected for the good of human civilisation. It also means that, in the near future, we will go extinct.

We are being naturally selected out of the population. Just like the squirrels and water deer, just like the sparrows and pheasants, gradually and inconspicuously our numbers dwindle. They say that no one predicted we would ever get to the point of dying out. This was because we were once so commonplace, so numerous. These days it sounds like a far-fetched legend, but at one time we made up half the world's population. Back then, we were simply 'human women', who were able to establish themselves and thrive anywhere on earth.

But in today's ecosystem, we are a frail race. Left to our devices to live anywhere and in any which way, we would be murdered or 'gobbled' within the day. That's why they say we require special protection, supervision and education. Young individuals like us, in particular, need to undergo adaptive training before we are released into the ecosystem.

Or, at least, that's how we learned it. From all the scientists, government employees and teachers who instructed us at the shelter.

They weren't the ones who taught us that 'gobble' was a metaphor for rape, though. Our sunbaes, the older girls, did.

We girls of the shelter heard many things from our sunbaes. Most of it was unverifiable, like Yeoreum's knowledge, but it was far more plausible than anything she said. There were legends passed on through word of mouth, rumours of unknown origin, warnings and predictions about what we would encounter in the outside world. Much of it was sexual in nature. We heard that, in the outside world, men were beleaguered by their lust for us. We heard that they bought and sold us for astronomical prices. That if we were ever captured by men like that, we would be locked up with no chance of escape and forced to have sex every day. A few of our sunbaes had appeared in pornos shot by men like that. Several of them had even seen those pornos with their own eyes, and, one time during history class, one sunbae who was supposed to present launched the wrong media file by mistake and the whole class saw it . . . 'It was horrible, but apparently she was pretty,' said Shiyoon, the girl who'd told us that story, who was our age. 'They said she looked super-pretty in that video,' she whispered to us in secret, looking frightened but at the same time oddly excited.

Whenever Yeoreum heard those kinds of rumours, she trembled in fear. She blinked her large eyes and her face went pale as if she were witnessing such a sight in real life, and she would clutch my sleeve tight. Shiyoon found Yeoreum's reaction amusing and would make her story more immersive, more obscene, more exaggerated. 'They said normally men are ten times stronger than us, but when they're raping us they get *thirty* times stronger.' 'They said there are really handsome men too, and that the scientists and teachers we talk to here are all ugly nerds. Men that are actually handsome are completely different.' 'Some men supposedly have muscles that are so toned that touching them feels like touching metal.' 'They said if you get married to a man like that, you're in for thrilling nights . . .'

Shiyoon, who was the closest among us to the sunbaes, diligently spread rumours of that flavour. During our lunchtime, and our break time, and our evening walk time, she chattered non-stop while the girls surrounded her and listened closely to her descriptions of 'thrilling nights'. Their blood was stirred by the allure of men's muscles, men's appearances, men's physical prowess on display. And if one of us perhaps did not encounter a good man, if a scandal broke that one of us had gotten captured by a bad man, they relished the incident even as it frightened them, like it was a horror story.

That's right. For them, it was only a horror story. Because they believed a scandal like that would never happen to them. They believed at face value that if they did everything the scientists, government officials and teachers at the shelter told them to do, they would come of age and be able to marry and leave the place. For the shelter had promised that they would pair us with good men worthy of having precious, beautiful girls of a rare race such as us as their wives. That men who had passed a rigorous and complicated government screening process would come to whisk us away. That they would bring us into the real

8

world; that they would protect us and cherish us forever; and that they would make us happy.

I didn't really join in with the other girls' conversations. In the dorms, before we went to sleep at night, when the others exchanged whispers in the dark, I simply listened. And when they closed their eyes and fantasised about their future husbands, I fantasised about something else.

'How do I escape from this place?'

Every night, I deliberated over my method of escape from the shelter. It was an old pastime and secret of mine. One that I didn't even reveal to Yeoreum.

I didn't consider what I would do after escaping. I had no concrete plans about how I would survive or where I would go. I simply studied and pondered over my escape route like solving a puzzle, like it was part of my daily routine. When was the shelter's surveillance at its most lax? What passageways would lead me outside? How, and with what tools, would I dismantle the locking mechanism? Whom among the girls could I trust and whom could I not? What other dangers lurked? Those were the questions that kept me going through the day.

A secret confers mental strength. For example, when I was in history class with a teacher I absolutely despised – when he taught us the process by which girls like us were being naturally selected out of the population and carved into our minds just what inferior beings we were – I was able to block him out and lose myself in deducing the code to release the locking mechanism at the shelter entrance. And during our physicals, while we received all sorts of exams and tests for completely unknown reasons, while we were injected with drugs of unknown purpose, while meticulous notes on the development of our bodies were made in our charts – while those doctors and scientists acted high-and-mighty like they knew everything there was to know about our bodies – I was able to laugh at them in secret. 'You don't know a thing. I'm going to stab you all in the back and run off. That's what's going to happen.'

I certainly wasn't the only one who wanted to leave the shelter. All the girls wanted to leave as early as they possibly could; they were bored and frustrated, having lived their whole lives locked/up here. But girls like Shiyoon believed their future would rescue them – a future in which they, in accordance with the established rules, graduated from the shelter and married a man from the outside world. But I did not want that future either. I didn't just want to escape from my present; I wanted to escape from that future too. Not only did I *not* want to become some man's possession and live a powerless life once more in need of 'protection', the last thing I wanted was to give birth to a daughter with such a man. If I did, that daughter would be classified a Class 1 Protected Minority Race like me and be forcibly sent to this shelter. That was the law. I would have to cut myself off from her, leaving her only with a paltry body that resembled mine and the name I gave her, like my mother did with me. I would have no choice but to send her here, this shelter that had been my personal hell all throughout childhood.

The government said that we 'contributed' to the genetic diversity of humankind like it was a really great thing. If that's what greatness was, I didn't want to become great. I just wanted to escape it all. But the reason I could not, the reason I had not even attempted to escape from the shelter though it was nearly time for me to graduate, was because of Yeoreum.

I felt guilty even just imagining, every night, leaving Yeoreum behind and running off by myself. Timid Yeoreum. Tender Yeoreum. Innocent Yeoreum who was suffused with useless hope. If I were to leave, she might die right away, unable to last another hour. If I were not there to watch her, she might vanish into thin air. Like the season that was her namesake. Like the extinct animals she loved so much.

The shelter consisted of three clean but old buildings. They were used for the girls' education, room and board, medical care and research, as well as for administration-only purposes.

West of the shelter was a mountain. It was open to us so we could go on field trips, have outdoor classes or go on walks, but halfway up the mountain there was a tall iron fence that we could not go beyond.

To the east was a highway. On it, cars that were like massive, bizarre-looking monsters roared by at incredible speeds, night and day. Across the highway – it was hard to tell because it was far away – it looked like there was an industrial complex, densely packed with a research institute and a number of factories. And, sure enough, obstructing the shelter from the highway was the tall iron fence.

To the north and south were the front and back entrances to the shelter respectively. Both of those were, unsurprisingly, very thoroughly secured, for they were built into enormous concrete walls that stretched to either side. Whatever was on the other side was blocked from view; even from the rooftops of the shelter buildings we could not see what lay beyond the north and south walls.

Thus the only things we were able to see of the outside world were the bleak trees of the mountain behind us and the highway to the east, factories barely visible beyond it. Whenever I had a spare moment, I took a look at the iron fence boxing us in in those two directions. The fence served to keep us from 'losing our way' while also protecting us from any outside trespassers. In other words, it was so tall and sturdy that we wouldn't be able to scale it even with the strength of a full-grown man. I was among the taller of my peers, but the fence was three times my height.

But I knew the fence's weakness.

I had looked over every inch of the shelter. I had examined the fence, the wall, the surveillance cameras, the security system and every angle of the locking mechanism. Thanks to years of relentless observation, I was able to envision all of them as distinctly as I could the pattern on my own bedsheets – so much so that if I closed my eyes, a map of the shelter automatically unfolded inside my head. I was able to see myself traversing the map and escaping too.

Even as I did things that could have aroused suspicion, on the outside I pretended to be a model student. Or, perhaps, it was precisely *because* I was going around doing suspicious things that I was able to be such a model student. As I said, secrets confer mental strength. The possibility that I'd be able to escape, telling myself that I could leave at any time if need be – that's what gave me the power to endure life at the shelter.

Now that I think of it, each of us endured that life in our own way. By doing something over and over.

Shiyoon, for instance, kept telling stories about men.

I kept planning my escape.

And Yeoreum. Yeoreum, of course, kept searching for traces of animals.

While I was investigating the iron fence, Yeoreum was absorbed in investigating the mountain behind the shelter. In her search for animal tracks, she went around industriously examining the dirt, trees and stones. Eventually she became just as much an expert of the mountain as I was of the security system, but getting to that point was a treacherous process. Even though the mountain sloped gradually and wasn't much to look at, because Yeoreum was slight and frail she injured herself many times while wandering about. It was common for her to lose her footing and fall or tumble off boulders. She would even get stung while pushing her way past insect nests and poked by thorny brambles. Whenever that happened, I was the one who made sure she was okay. I was used to taking care of Yeoreum when she was hurt, nursing her when she was ill, indulging her when she acted like a baby and telling her, firmly, not to make mistakes like that again.

There was even a time that Yeoreum went missing on the mountain. I was thoroughly baffled. It was like she'd gone missing in her own backyard. She was found in a far-off thicket, fast asleep under the shade of a tree. With something like an ugly, withered seed pod clutched protectively in her hand.

Yeoreum claimed that the seed pod was strong evidence of water deer living close by. I didn't listen too closely so I don't remember the exact details, but she said that those plants were food to the water deer, and that she'd uncovered actual traces of the water deer having eaten them.

Yeoreum liked water deer. Out of all the old extinct animals she had learned about, she liked water deer best. According to her, the water deer were a kind of herbivorous deer that had populated the earth along with other members of the deer family throughout the Quaternary Period of the Cenozoic Era, but the water deer had their own unique, intriguing characteristics distinct from their relatives. First, while other cervid males had crown-like horns representing their maleness, neither male nor female water deer grew horns. Furthermore, unlike the average deer that we imagined to be meek and skittish, water deer were aggressive and curious. In fact, with their two huge tusks protruding from their mouths and the terrifying banshee-like screams they'd let out while active at night, or their tendency to appear out of nowhere and startle people, the water deer were rather threatening creatures. 'They have long and graceful necks and legs. They like swimming and they run around with such energy and vigour.' Yeoreum described the water deer as if she had seen them with her own eyes.

I think I knew why Yeoreum felt such a special affection toward the water deer. She never admitted it herself but it was easy enough to guess. Yeoreum probably thought the circumstances of the water deer, an animal of the past, were similar to her own – hundreds of thousands of a kind once alive and thriving, but after some point sharply declining in number until, finally, vanishing without a trace. If one such animal had managed to survive until now, it would be a living time capsule of sorts for retaining the characteristics of mammals long past; it would become a valuable research subject for academics. Just like us girls, it would be seen as a rare and mysterious creature.

We had always been rare and mysterious creatures. We'd been taught this ever since we were children. After the development of artificial wombs, all other human women had chosen their own comfort and strength and gotten rid of their uteruses, undergone genetic modification, received stem cell transplants, replaced their organs and received life-extending medication. All other human women had passed on new genes to their daughters and become ancestors to a newly evolved human race. But our mothers were different. They'd either been unable to make that choice because they were too poor, or they'd refused that choice because of some ancient religious and moral belief, or they'd carried on living in a 'nature-friendly' manner in the hinterlands without any exposure to scientific technology. We were the daughters of such women.

I sometimes imagined the lives of evolved women. What was it like to live a life of not needing to suffer through menses, or pregnancy, or childbirth? What was it like to live a life of being able to go anywhere you wanted, of not needing to be protected by anyone, of not being overpowered by anyone? What was it like to live a life of not being ashamed of your body? I ached to be reborn as an evolved woman in my next life. But never once did I see myself as some plant-eating animal that died out even before we did. Yeoreum's pastime felt extremely morbid to me.

The incident happened at the turn of the season. Around the time the quiet season transitioned into the windy season and the stillness was broken every once in a while by sudden gusts of wind. It was about a month until our graduation exam and everyone was in high spirits.

Our graduation exam was not a big deal. It was when the men who had applied for a wife among us and passed the government's criteria met with us personally and made their choice. In other words, it was the time they selected their wife-to-be. We didn't have much to prepare. We simply had to show those men that we were ready to adapt to human society and that we were healthy enough to get pregnant and give birth. Of course, sexual attraction was critical too, but the shelter severely restricted how we adorned ourselves, saying that it was unethical (I'm not exactly sure *why* it was considered unethical). So, the girls would bring out their homely accessories and the make-up they had snuck in without the teachers knowing and discuss late into the night how they could make themselves look pretty in the most subtle way.

But that night, things were quiet. This was because it was time for lights-out and Shiyoon still hadn't returned to the dorms. Without Shiyoon, who would've given everyone random advice on men and looking pretty, the conversation kept drying up. And so the girls went back to topics they'd discussed to death in the past and even dragged Yeoreum and me, who normally didn't or couldn't participate, into it.

'What sort of man do you wish will choose you?' they asked us. This was after all of them had shared their ideal type at length numerous times.

I had to swallow the urge to tell them they'd probably be incredibly disappointed when they came face-to-face with the eligible bachelors. 'I shouldn't do anything to cause suspicion. Because I'll be out of here soon enough.' I meditated on my personal mantra and made up something appropriate. I hope he's someone who's kind and understanding, someone with such-and-such colour hair, who's this many years old, something like that (I don't even remember).

But Yeoreum wasn't good at lying like that.

'I . . .' Wide-eyed, she met the gazes of all the girls staring at her and grew lost in thought. Then, haltingly, she replied, 'I hope it's a man from a land where summer exists.'

Everyone started giggling. Someone even snorted blatantly.

I felt myself grow strangely angry.

'I'm serious. I'd be happy with that . . . I think I can definitely be that person's wife and the mother of his sons in that case.'

Yeoreum was completely earnest but the girls burst out laughing again.

That's how compliant Yeoreum was. She'd practically committed to memory what the teachers taught us: 'As one man's wife and as a mother, you will play a major role in this world.' She was the only girl who took such an old-fashioned lesson seriously. However, apart from the administrators of the shelter, she was more or less afraid of men from the outside world and she couldn't seem to fathom what it meant, specifically, to live the life of someone's wife and someone's mother. Her imagination dwelled only in an unrealistic dimension, on things like animals of old, her mother and the wilderness of a foreign land.

Unable to bear it any longer, I dragged Yeoreum to the public restroom and confronted her. 'What the hell are you on about? Can't you see that everyone's laughing at you because you keep acting that way? Don't tell me you're planning on spouting idiotic answers like that during your exam?'

Flustered, Yeoreum blinked at me. With the meek eyes of a herbivore. 'What do you mean, "that way"?'

'It's like you're on another planet. The stuff you're saying is completely removed from reality. I'm telling you, this is the *only* place anyone will think you're being cute. Men from the outside world? They're going to wonder where we even found someone as weird as you. Not to mention, you have a weak body and scored the lowest out of all of us in physical development. What are you going to do if no one picks you? What if no one comes to take you away in the end? And, at the last minute, some creepy loser gets his paws on you?'

In my head I knew it was coming out all wrong, but I couldn't stop myself. I was always losing my cool in front of her, always blurting out remarks that cut her.

Yeoreum hunched her shoulders tightly, crestfallen. 'Still,' she said softly, 'it's all right.' The *ddok-ddok* sound of water dripping to the floor, leaking somewhere in the restroom, was louder than her voice. 'Because the govern-ment is supposed to be really strict in their screening . . . I'm sure even girls like me will meet a good man.'

'Do you seriously believe that? You know that's not possible. Sure, maybe you won't get bums and alcoholics coming your way. But out of the ones that do, you've got to be able to *choose* the man who's going to treat you better, the man who's got all his brain cells working, who's got some sense. You've got to know to *like* the right person, is what I'm saying! You've got to get the hang of that sort of thing yourself. I can't always be there next to you, taking care of you.'

'I know, okay? I know people don't like me very much. And I know you don't either . . .'

'Yeoreum, how many times do I have to tell you, when someone gives you advice because they're worried about you, just take it as advice, okay? If I didn't like you, why would I try to give you advice in the first place?'

Yeoreum gazed sadly at me. 'I want to do that too. Just take it as advice, think about it rationally . . . Wouldn't it be great if I could be as tall and strong as you and knew all the tricks of the trade?'

I started to say something, but Yeoreum's next words left me speechless.

'I bet the water deer are exactly like you.'

At that moment we heard footsteps outside the restroom rapidly approaching in our direction. Teachers, it seemed like.

Hastily, I pulled Yeoreum into the supply closet to hide. Looking back on it, I'm not sure why I did that. It was against the rules to wander around after lights-out, but using the restroom was still allowed. I think I was more jumpy about our conversation than about the rules – I was scared the teachers might hear.

However, we were not the ones having a conversation that shouldn't be overheard. The teachers were.

'And the body?'

We glanced at each other, alarmed by those words, then held our breaths and listened. The two teachers who had entered the restroom closed the outer door and continued whispering, voices grim.

'They were able to retrieve it in good condition, thankfully. It didn't look like anyone had disturbed it.'

'That's a relief, at least. In many cases we've not even been able to find a body.'

'How on earth are we supposed to tell the girls that Shiyoon's dead?'

Yeoreum let out a tiny scream. I quickly pressed a hand against her lips. Fortunately the teachers had turned on the faucets and didn't seem to hear us over the sound of the flowing water and their own voices. In that cramped space, holding each other tight, we overheard the whole shocking tale.

Shiyoon had tried to escape from the shelter and died.

She had scaled the iron fence. The same iron fence that I had observed plenty of times but had never actually tried to climb. She had climbed that fence and gone outside. And then, while crossing the highway naked, she had been run over by a car and killed.

'I'm puzzled, frankly. I thought Shiyoon of all people

would adjust incredibly well to the standard marriage process . . . She'd been looking forward to her graduation exam day for years.'

At this teacher's words, the other sighed. He was the teacher I didn't like, the one that taught history class. He was really old and uptight, and the sort of teacher who acted ice-cold in all situations.

'Girls are, by their very nature, unpredictable. We must never let our guard down or put our trust in them. No matter how normal they look, they are closer to being primitive beasts of the wild. I do wonder that we bring them to a place like this and attempt to socialise them quite in vain.'

The younger teacher let out a groan. Then, after the sound of water sloshing, we heard the outer door to the restroom swing open.

'You're not wrong. And this isn't the first time we've had an accident like this. Wouldn't it be better if we just warned the girls? Tell them that they could get killed trying to cross the highway so they'd best not get any ideas . . . ?'

'We can't do that. How would we explain it to them? We've told them that those things called *cars* are equipped with a self-driving system but that there's absolutely no risk of accidents so they can set their minds at ease.'

'I know it's awkward, but this does keep happening year after year . . .'

We heard the sounds of the teachers' footsteps grow distant as the door shut. Then silence once again filled the restroom.

I was stunned. I couldn't comprehend what I had just

heard. To think that Shiyoon, of all people, had attempted an escape. And not just that – there were girls who tried to escape every year and the majority of them died. They didn't even make it very far from the shelter. They were run over by cars and killed right under our noses . . .

I didn't even know how to process such absurdity. I only felt a dull fury. The teachers' conversation had been far too relaxed, too ordinary. They had even dared to chuckle while they spoke, as if Shiyoon's death had been nothing more than an everyday occurrence, as if they found our foolishness amusing.

'Shiyoon had a lover,' Yeoreum whispered into my chest. She was crying. 'She was secretly seeing a man from the outside world. She probably climbed the iron fence to meet him.'

Yeoreum's body trembled violently as she wept. It didn't even occur to me to comfort her. Blankly, I said, 'You're joking. How do you know that?'

Yeoreum looked up at me once, then quickly turned away. She stepped away from my chest, saying, 'Shiyoon told me. She thought out of all of us I'd be the one to believe her . . .'

The teachers lied and told us that Shiyoon was sick all of a sudden and had been transferred to a hospital. It was a big hospital, so we wouldn't be able to see her for a while. The girls were taken aback but seemed to accept this explanation; they had no reason to believe otherwise. Yeoreum and I deliberately withheld the truth from them. We held our tongues. And we thought about the body that we weren't able to see, that we'd never be able to see. No. We thought about the bodies.

*Fortunately it didn't look like anyone had disturbed the body. In many cases we're not even able to find a body.* I couldn't get the teachers' words out of my head. What did it mean to 'disturb' a body? Where had the bodies they 'weren't even able to find' gone? Had someone taken them?

It was horrifying to think about. I was scared, but also angry. Terror and rage seemed to be two sides of the same coin for me. When I flipped my rage over, there was terror; when I flipped my terror over, rage was back. I was angry at the cars that had killed Shiyoon. I was angry at myself for not knowing what *cars* were exactly. I had no clue how cars moved, or what a 'self-driving system' was, or how something we were told was safe could turn out not to be safe at all. I was so terribly curious about this secret that our teachers didn't tell us, but I had no one to ask. What do you need to do to *not* be run over by a car? Or is that not possible? Is everyone who crosses the highway bound to die?

I had spent such a long time chewing over how to escape the shelter and yet I had no plans for what to do once I was over the fence. I couldn't believe myself. How could I have failed to consider that?

The windy season was closing in. The wind began blowing fiercely night after night, and outside our windows the trees swayed and shed their leaves. When the leaves of the trees that grew densely all over the garden and the mountain behind the shelter brushed against each other all at once, their noisy rustling buried the sounds of the cars racing along the highway beyond the iron fence. At least that was good.

Yeoreum and I became complete strangers to each other. Maybe it was because of our argument in the restroom that day or the effect Shiyoon's death had had on her, but Yeoreum stealthily avoided me and I couldn't bring myself to speak to her either. Sometimes I saw Yeoreum sniffling, weeping by herself, but I couldn't even console her – because I didn't know what sort of conversations she had shared with Shiyoon all this time nor how close the two of them had been.

I suppose I felt a bit betrayed as well. I had thought I was Yeoreum's only friend until then.

Such was the state we were in when we took our graduation exam. After the eligible bachelors looked through materials that precisely detailed our bodies, intelligence, temperament and other characteristics, they chose a few candidates they wanted to meet face to face. Then they called forth each candidate one by one into the interview room and spoke with them for ten minutes. That was our graduation exam.

I was included in the first batch of candidates.

I didn't want to do the face-to-face interview. I was filled with more distrust than ever and felt an unthinkable outrage that I was turning my life over to a man under the pretext of marriage. The government said they were highly selective when screening the qualifications of the men who would become our husbands, but what if those 'qualifications' were – just like a car's supposed 'self-driving system' – imperfect and questionable? What if those men pretended they'd be good husbands and then sold us off for a high price somewhere? What if they kept us locked up and forced us to have sex with them every day? What if they made us appear in a porno? *Normally men are ten times stronger than us, but when they're raping us they get thirty times stronger.* Unexpectedly, I recalled the horror story I'd heard from Shiyoon. All those stories she'd told us that I'd only half-listened to, that I didn't even know I still remembered – all those stories came flooding back to me and my heart clenched.

Still, I had no choice but to go to the interview room and face this so-called eligible bachelor. As soon as I saw the man, I immediately regained my composure.

He did not look terrifying. He wasn't weird-looking, or large and muscular, or particularly handsome. He looked like any one of the teachers or government employees or scientists who were in charge of us. He seemed no different from any of the adults we'd interacted with at the shelter over the years. Those middle-aged men who were overconfident for no reason, carefree for no reason. Those complacent, lazy, indifferent ahjussis.

The girls who were waiting for a man who was exceptionally handsome would be disappointed, that much was obvious. I kept answering the man's questions in a bland, unenthusiastic way. What are your likes and dislikes; what do you think of your mother; what is the first thing you want to do in the outside world; what does a great marriage look like to you . . . I knew all the 'ideal' answers to those types of question but I didn't want to respond in the way I'd been taught. At my brusque, impertinent replies, the man was more than a little perplexed.

The interview ended quickly. That was the first and last time I messed up the exam on purpose. I was in a good mood and feeling oddly satisfied. While the next batch of girls were doing their interviews, I meandered about the garden and listened to the sound of the wind. I looked at the trees and flowers I'd seen my whole life with new eyes and realised, for the first time, that I might never see those plants again. I wondered who among us that unremarkable man would choose as his bride.

The results were revealed that evening. The first one to pass her graduation exam was Yeoreum.

'She's his type.'

That's what the counsellor said, plain and simple, when I asked him how on earth Yeoreum had been chosen.

'His *type*?' I repeated flatly.

'He said he's into girls like Yeoreum. You know, girls who are small and pale. Ditzy, thin. Fascinating, isn't it? I think he said they seemed like fairies?' The counsellor shrugged, chuckling.

I did not find this fascinating at all.

'But . . . you said Yeoreum didn't respond with any of the right answers. And she still passed the exam? I don't under-stand. What was the point of everything we learned over the years, then?'

Only then did the counsellor truly look at me in earnest. He gave me a strange, resigned look. It was the type of look I hated, one that the teachers were always giving us.

A look that said a girl like me wouldn't understand even if she had everything explained to her. A haughty attitude that said the secrets of the world could not be divulged to creatures like us who weren't even human, who had ceased to be human, who were far too inferior, too incomplete, too foolish to be considered human.

'Well, it worked out in the end, didn't it? It'll be a weight off your chest. All of us knew how worried you were that Yeoreum wouldn't graduate. You must be relieved now.'

I could say nothing.

The counsellor was right. I should be feeling relief now. All this time, I had been sick to my stomach with worry for Yeoreum. I'd feared she would fade away more and more from the real world, lost in her own childish fantasy. Because she was frail and careless, my nerves were always on edge that one day she would be killed somewhere in some sort of accident. But now that Yeoreum had safely graduated, I should finally be able to set my heart at ease. I should be able to congratulate her and be happy for her, that 'as one man's wife and as a mother, she will be able to play a major role in this world.'

But I could not.

I wanted to tell her congratulations. I wanted to walk up to Yeoreum, who was puzzled by the news that she had passed, and tell her she did great. But throughout our lunchtime, break time and dinnertime she was constantly surrounded by the other girls. The girls asked her over and over how on earth she'd gotten the man to like her and what they had talked about during the interview. How was she feeling? Had it sunk in yet? She better keep in touch.

She better enjoy all the pretty clothes and fancy theatres and yummy food . . . Even the younger girls crowded ceaselessly around Yeoreum and made a huge fuss.

I had just one thing I wanted to ask her. I wanted to ask her if that man lived in a place where a season called summer existed.

I could only watch Yeoreum from a distance. She had a peculiar look on her face that was a bit dazed, a bit pleased, a bit sad. When our eyes met, she looked away hastily. That hurt. It was like she had cast me off and was heading toward her own life, to the world of evolved humans, to her future as a wife and mother – while I had turned into a ghost, still entangled in our old relationship. Without my even realising it, Yeoreum had suddenly grown up, with her own secrets held close to her chest. She had become someone I did not recognise at all.

That evening, I went back to the dorms early and buried myself under the covers of my bed. I had started my period that day too, as if things couldn't get any worse. With my stomach aching and blood flowing out of me, I pulled the quilt over my head and sobbed. I was ashamed of my body and ashamed of my heart. Even in the midst of my breakdown, I remembered that Yeoreum always suffered from far more severe menstrual pain than I did and that her cycle was always irregular, and I worried whether she'd be able to give birth safely with a body like that. Like a fool, I could not easily let go of that worry.

The next morning, I rose early and went to the mountain. I couldn't stand to stay inside. I walked up the path that Yeoreum and I had always taken and examined the grassy thickets and the tree bark and the undersides of rocks just like Yeoreum had. Looking for the droppings and tracks of rats, dogs, cats, raccoons, squirrels, rabbits, roe deer and water deer. Looking for the feathers and bones of sparrows, pigeons, pheasants, magpies and crows. But I didn't know how to find them, or what animal traces looked like. And in this season of fierce windiness, it didn't seem like anything would've been left behind anyway. This way and that way, the grass and bushes and trees all swayed together, singing. When a strong wind blew, the whole mountain itself seemed to tremble.

That's why I didn't hear the footsteps of someone following me. When Yeoreum grabbed my arm, I jumped in surprise and whirled around.

'Why are you walking so fast? Didn't you hear me calling you?'

Yeoreum looked up at me, panting, her face flushed bright red. I was so startled that for a moment I simply stared at her, motionless.

When I didn't say anything, Yeoreum swallowed. Anxiety was written all over her face. 'I—I'm leaving tomorrow. The man who's going to be my husband is going to pick me up. They said I just need to pack my belongings. Not that I have much to pack.'

'Okay. Congrats,' I blurted. My tone was curt in spite of myself.

'So what will you do now?'

'What do you mean?'

'You're going to escape, right? Like you planned?'

This time, I was so surprised my whole body recoiled. But Yeoreum just looked puzzled at my reaction.

All these years, I thought I had kept my plan to escape a secret from Yeoreum, but she'd known everything like it had been obvious from the very beginning. So obvious that she hadn't even thought of it as a secret.

'I dunno,' I replied vaguely. 'Probably.'

But the reality was I hadn't thought at all about escaping over the past several days. Escape had only ever been a nebulous daydream. Never once had I dared even to muster the resolve to turn that daydream into reality. Not like Shiyoon. I was too scared to try. I'd told myself that I couldn't leave because I was worried about Yeoreum, but that was just an excuse. I didn't have the courage, or the will, to run off into a world that I did not know.

'I see,' Yeoreum said in a trembling voice. She let go of my arm and grasped both of my hands. She looked like she was carefully choosing the right words to say something painful. 'I . . . I wanted to say thank you before I left. For staying here because of me.'

I stared blankly at her. My every nerve was focused on Yeoreum's hands. Her skin was soft, yet cold. Mysteriously soft, mysteriously cold. I wondered if, perhaps, this was what a late-summer breeze blowing from the north would have felt like, long ago when we still had four seasons. I wanted to take the feeling of her grasp and tuck it into my pocket for safekeeping. So she wouldn't be able to run off anywhere.

'It must've been so annoying being here because of

me . . . I know you really hate it here and you probably wanted to leave as soon as possible, but you held yourself back for so long for my sake. I—I really tried my best. To graduate properly and get married, to be someone who can take care of herself . . . I thought about it really hard. About how I need to be someone's wife and someone's mother, how that's the path that's been set for me . . . Because then you'll be able to leave here with peace of mind.'

Tears welled in Yeoreum's bloodshot eyes but she managed to keep herself from crying. 'Now you can go, you don't have to worry about me. I . . . I'll find happiness too.'

The peculiar, incomprehensible look on Yeoreum's face from the past few days – the one that had made her seem like she was somewhere far away – was clear for the first time. Suddenly, everything came into focus. Like the whole world had sharpened. Like even the wind had fallen still. Like the cats and rabbits and water deer and pigeons and magpies and owls were all listening quietly to our conversation.

I squeezed Yeoreum's hand back.

'Don't get married, Yeoreum. Let's escape this place together.'

Yeoreum blinked and the tears that had gathered in her eyes rolled down her cheeks.

With a hand, I brushed her tears away. 'I can't leave without you.'

There was no time. Since Yeoreum's husband-to-be was coming the following morning to take her away, we had to escape that very night. We gave up on any elaborate preparation and had no choice but to go forth blindly, trusting in the plan I'd had in my head for all those years.

It would be fully possible to get off the shelter property. There was no doubt in my mind about that. The problem was the highway. I had no idea what we needed to do to avoid the cars and there was no chance I'd find out. The conversation we'd overheard between those teachers in the restroom kept going round and round in my head. I could imagine their taunting words, saying it hasn't even been a week since Shiyoon died and already another incident's happened and, well, no wonder those Class I Protected Minority Race girls are so stupid and reckless. They're closer to being primitive beasts.

I was terrified that we would die in vain. Not just because of the highway: I couldn't fathom what sort of dangers lurked in the outside world. It was one thing if it were just me, but I was scared I might rob Yeoreum of her life. But at the same time, because Yeoreum was by my side, I had made a firm resolution: I could not send Yeoreum to that man and Yeoreum could not leave me behind. And, so, it was better to die.

We packed lightly and waited for lights-out. In the dead of night, when everyone was asleep, we slipped out of the dorms.

I smashed the security cameras in the hallway. And, of course, I had already figured out a safe route that would avoid all the guards on patrol. I even knew the code that would release the locking mechanism of the front entrance. I worried that they might have changed the code after Shiyoon's escape, but thankfully it was still the same.

We were able to exit the building with ease. Almost unbelievably so. Everything was exactly as it had been in my mental simulation. Staying hidden in the shadows of the building, we stole across the front lawn of the shelter. Now, if we could just climb the iron fence surrounding the shelter property, our escape would be a success.

The fence had two weak points. One of them was a large hole on the side that faced the highway, large enough that girls of our size could squeeze through to the other side. But I suspected that, since Shiyoon had probably used that hole for her escape, the shelter administrators had likely already discovered it and covered it up. Not to mention, if we went in that direction, we'd inevitably have to cross the highway. I figured it was probably best to avoid that if possible.

And so we went up the mountain. Near the border of the fence there, two large rocks were stacked on top of each other. I thought if we could use those rocks as steps, we'd manage to climb over the fence. Yeoreum was short so it would be a challenge for her, but if I could boost her up with my hands, I thought she'd be able to make it.

But when we arrived at the spot, the rocks were smaller than I remembered.

I looked back and forth from Yeoreum to the fence. 'Can you do this?'

At a glance, the fence was incredibly high. Yeoreum's face was pale. She was already exhausted and breathless from us hurrying as fast as we could from the dormitory building and up the mountain, concealing traces of ourselves as we went.

'I can do this. I can do this,' Yeoreum muttered, more to herself than to me, nodding resolutely. I was concerned but put out my hands to grasp the bottom of her foot anyway.

The moment I felt her weight, I thought my arm was going to crook inwards. I strained my muscles and held Yeoreum up in the air. Her body teetered. I resisted the urge to shout and urged her in a whisper, 'Hurry! Now, hurry!'

Yeoreum's arms flailed and she grabbed the top of the iron fence. I was going to grab her legs and give her a push upward, but she didn't even manage to hold on for a second before she let go. I caught her as she fell and the two of us collapsed to the ground.

'See, what'd I tell you? Didn't I tell you to exercise regularly?'

'Sorry . . .'

'Never mind. Let's try again.'

I helped Yeoreum up. In the moonlight, her face looked even paler. The wind was blowing so strongly that her hair was flying around in a tangled mess. I forced a smile and told her it was okay, she didn't have to be nervous, as I stroked her back. And then, once more, I supported the bottom of her foot with my hand.

We tried five or six times. But no matter what we did, we were unsuccessful. If anything, the more we tried, the more the energy started draining out of both of us. It seemed like we wouldn't be able to get over the fence like this.

Despair closed in on us. We couldn't afford to fail after

coming this far. I told Yeoreum this wasn't working and made her rest for a moment while I managed to find other things we could climb on top of: a wooden plank and wide, flat stones. I stacked them like a tower on top of the rocks and tried climbing up. But it still wasn't tall enough, so we decided to leave behind one of the bags we'd brought, adding it instead to the tower of stuff.

While we were in the middle of doing that, we heard footsteps at the base of the mountain and saw the shine of a flashlight cut through the air.

'Over there! They're over there!'

The two of us shot up like a gush of water at the same time.

All of a sudden, it seemed ridiculous that we hadn't succeeded before that moment. Like dancers performing a well-arranged choreography, we moved in perfect sync with one another. I climbed up the tower I had built and held my hands out to Yeoreum. Yeoreum stepped lightly into my hands and, the moment she found her centre of gravity, I pushed upward, and Yeoreum used the momentum to scramble right up to the top of the fence. I heard a thud and a short scream as Yeoreum dropped to the ground on the other side. I followed immediately by leaping up to grab the top of the fence and heaving my body upward, using the crossbeam as a foothold.

Just as my foot touched the top of the fence, I heard gunshots.

I was so shocked that I lost my balance and fell face first over the other side. Luckily there was a soft thicket of grass in that spot so it didn't hurt too badly. But Yeoreum seemed to have sprained her ankle, for she was clutching her leg and groaning.

'Are you all right?'

Yeoreum nodded, staring with wide eyes at the other side of the fence. 'Was that a gun?'

'I-It's probably a tranquilliser gun,' I said uncertainly.

The shelter treated us like precious, irreplaceable resources – surely they wouldn't senselessly shoot us dead just because we tried to run away, I thought. But there was no way to know for certain.

Yeoreum hobbled to her feet. 'Let's hurry.'

'Will you be all right?'

'We need to go . . . We've made it this far, haven't we? Hurry.'

I swallowed my guilt and helped Yeoreum lean against me.

We were now in a new world. Although we'd climbed this mountain too many times to count, we had never stepped foot in this part. I illuminated the darkness with the flashlight I'd brought and focused all my energy on not losing our way. At some point, that role shifted to Yeoreum. She didn't know where we were going either, but at least she was more familiar with the mountain than I was.

We kept looking behind us as we walked. Because of Yeoreum's leg, our pace was far too slow. We were sick to our stomachs with fear that bullets might come flying toward us at any moment. But the wind was so loud that we couldn't hear much of anything. Over the sound of the leaves rustling, I thought I could hear shouts somewhere far in the distance, but I couldn't be sure.

'I'm sorry . . .'

Between her gasps of breath, Yeoreum's voice was
choked with tears. Her body leaning against my shoulder
was slowly getting heavier.

I clenched my teeth and babbled uselessly in response.
'We don't have time for your tears right now.'

'But . . .'

'I told you, stop snivelling. Hurry up and keep looking
for a path.'

Yeoreum fell silent. Slowly, silently, our feet moved.
Eventually a downhill path appeared before us and it looked
like we would be able to get off the mountain.

The wind grew steadily louder – so loud I thought we
would go deaf. Almost as if a typhoon were brewing. At
first I was anxious that the wind would prevent us from
getting our bearings, but, little by little, we became used
to it. With noise like this, our enemies wouldn't be able to
hear the sound we were making. As if the sound itself were
hiding us.

As we kept walking, the dirt path became firmer and
wider. It had been tamped down by people's footsteps over
many, many years. Soon we would be at the base of the
mountain. What came after that? What would we do after
that? I was gripped with excitement and terror at the same
time. But then, all of a sudden, a different kind of terror
seized me.

I could not feel the wind on my skin.

The wind was not blowing. At some point, our hair and
clothing had stopped fluttering. I could not feel the gusts
of air that had been beating at my skin. The air had gone

as still as indoors. But the trees were shaking. The trees on either side of the path shook and rustled their leaves.

'Y-Yeoreum, hang on. This—'

'We're almost at the base!'

Yeoreum dragged me forward, hurrying. She descended almost like she was tumbling down the path. Before long, after we'd pushed past overgrown brambles and turned a corner, a wide-open space opened up abruptly before us.

It was the highway.

We stood there, frozen. In front of us, cars like massive monsters barrelled past at incredible speed. Seeing the highway from here felt completely different from seeing it over the shelter's iron fence. These cars that passed by our very noses, with no barrier between us and them, were terrifyingly fast. When they were far away they didn't seem that fast, but the moment the cars were in front of us their velocity surged as if by some supernatural power. As they headed off into the distance they seemed to slow again somewhat, but before we knew it they vanished over the horizon. Every car repeated this process.

There was a field on the other side of the highway. A wide-open field growing some sort of green grass or crop we didn't know the name of. And, in the far distance, an inky forest floated like an island atop the field.

I thought my legs were going to give way. This was the end. Crossing the highway was impossible. We wouldn't be able to avoid these cars even if we were able to run at full speed; with Yeoreum's sprain, it was completely out of the question. What if I gave Yeoreum a piggyback ride? No, that was a death wish. What would we do? Wasn't there any way to get these cars to stop? My mind felt like it was going blank.

'This . . . How do we . . .'

When I opened my mouth, Yeoreum grabbed my arm and whispered, 'Shh! Look over there.'

I turned to look where Yeoreum was pointing.

It was the foothills on another part of the mountain we had just climbed down. The moment I saw the trees on those slopes, I remembered once more what the shock of seeing the highway had made me forget: there was still no wind, yet the trees were shaking. Like something was shaking them on purpose.

Something had suddenly appeared from between those trees.

On instinct, I pulled Yeoreum to me and held her close. At first I thought they were our enemies chasing us; the next moment I wondered if they were alien monsters from outer space. In the dim glow of the highway lights and the headlights of the cars, when I finally realised what those creatures were, maybe three seconds had passed. To me, it felt as long as three minutes.

They were water deer. The creatures that had emerged from the mountain were water deer.

Five water deer covered in glossy, nut-brown fur moved their long, graceful necks and legs and leaped nimbly to the side of the highway. Each one had long tusks protruding from the mouth; and like magnificent, priceless orna-ments of ivory, the tusks glinted, rounded semicircles in the moonlight. It was like seeing the regal warriors of an ancient tribe – warriors wrapped in soft yet sturdy animal hide, holding exquisite weaponry, more beautiful than useful. One water deer's clear, dark pupil looked right at Yeoreum and me.

Time seemed to stop.

Hardly daring to breathe, we stared at the water deer. And the water deer stared at us. With a serene, impassive gaze that gave us no hint as to what they were thinking, the water deer observed us. That gaze pierced us through and pinned us so we couldn't move a muscle. I was afraid that the slightest movement would startle them and they'd turn into a mirage and be scattered to the wind.

The water deer were the first to move.

One of them let out a bizarre wail that sounded both like a horn and like a human scream. Taking that to be the signal, all five water deer walked together onto the highway. Lightly and easily, the way a person might step onto their living room carpet.

Our hearts dropped to our stomachs and Yeoreum and I both screamed. But the accident we feared would happen did not. Once the water deer were in the middle of the highway, those violently speeding cars slowed down to a smooth stop as if by magic. One by one, the car doors opened and startled passengers began stepping out. All of them stared at the water deer, stupefied.

All the cars behind them stopped. The people stopped. Even the rustling of the trees ceased. In that hushed still-ness, the only creatures that moved were the water deer. They were crossing to the other side of the highway, as leis-urely as can be, as if ignoring the passing of time.

Yeoreum tugged on my sleeve. 'Let's follow them.'

I hesitated for a moment. Yeoreum looked full of conviction but for some reason I was afraid. I wasn't sure whether I was afraid to follow the water deer or afraid to step onto the highway, or if it was something else. It occurred to me that, if I had been alone, I would probably have remained frozen, unable to move even an inch until the animals had finished crossing the highway. But because Yeoreum was pulling me along with her, because, even though she was limping with that small body of hers, she was heading to the highway with such determination, I followed her.

Nothing moved at all as we crossed the highway with the water deer. Even the clouds in the sky seemed to be holding their position, gazing down on us.

At last, when Yeoreum and I stood on the kerb on the other side of the highway, I no longer looked behind me.

*Dedicated to the K-pop girl group Oh My Girl.*

# Rabi

Rabi was the only granddaughter of a shaman. Her life had been decided for her even before she was born. She would be the next shaman; there was to be no alternative. At least, that is what Rabi's grandmother believed.

In the olden days, the life allotted to Rabi would have been one of honour. Back in the age when her tribe in the tropics still lived by their long-held traditions and customs, that most certainly would have been the case. Back when their men went into the forest to hunt snakes and boar and catch fish, and their women wove clothing out of raffia and tree bark, and everyone shared the taro and sweet potatoes dug up from the earth. Back when they married, and went to war with, and traded crockery and ornaments and alcohol with, the neighbouring coastal tribes and river tribes. If now were anything like those days past, the shaman would hold grand festivals and perform ceremonial rituals for each season. She would bear responsibility for the life and death, joys and sorrows of all her people and she would be regarded, in turn, with both respect and awe. The sunshine and winds of the dry season and the clouds of the wet season all rested in the single flick of the shaman's wrist and the flutter of her skirt.

But these are not such times.

I have watched the shamans of this tribe for centuries. I have seen the mothers of the shaman family pass on their duties to their daughters and the daughters pass them on to their daughters. I have observed the faces of so many countless daughters resembling, or not resembling, their mothers and grandmothers. I have seen them all, remember them all. And amongst them all, Rabi was the most dissatisfied with her family's lot in life.

Rabi caused everyone grief from the moment she emerged from her mother's womb. Not only did she have a brawny body unlike a girl's, but because her umbilical cord had coiled itself around her arm, her mother suffered excruciating labour pains and died not half a day after giving birth to her. Rabi's grandmother was left with no choice but to raise her, but Rabi screamed and wailed so violently that her grandmother could hardly bear to ask Rabi's aunts to nurse her. As soon as Rabi learned to talk, she asked 'Why?' constantly. She doubted and challenged everything around her. Why did the flowers bloom? Why did it rain? Why did she keep getting lice no matter how many times she picked them out? Why did lizards stay alive even when you cut up their bodies? Why was the moon the moon and the sun the sun and Grandmother Grandmother and Rabi Rabi? Of course, the tribespeople passed on myths and legends from generation to generation, explaining the natural phenomena of the world and all the affairs of humans. And since shamans learned those stories by heart better than anyone, Rabi's grandmother had plenty of answers to tuck into the palms of

curious little children. But Rabi wasn't satisfied with any of
these stories. If Rabi's grandmother told Rabi one hundred
stories that she had heard as a little girl from her own
grandmother, Rabi in turn asked fifty questions and offered
fifty opinions of her own, as if to pay up for those stories
fair and square. Grandmother told Rabi she was being
insolent and scolded her, and without fail Rabi would lash
out. Grandmother got angry and belligerent toward Rabi;
not to be outdone, Rabi screamed and bawled. If Grandmother hit Rabi, Rabi quit crying and simply glowered with
venom in her eyes. When Rabi got into a temper like that,
Grandmother was sometimes afraid of her. It wasn't just
that Rabi was very curious or got into mischief. She looked
like she possessed a kind of spitefulness that could not be
undone, an inherent malice toward her origins, her family
pedigree and the rules of society. Rabi's grandmother, the
old shaman, had a bad feeling about her granddaughter.
Or rather, she had a bad feeling about the world that surrounded her.

The traditions of the tribe were on the road to inevit-
able collapse. Now, everyone used the official language and
followed the state religion or nothing at all. Only the old
shaman and a few of her generation had command of the
ancient tribal language. The rest could only comprehend
its vaguest context and the young people couldn't understand anything at all. To the young people, the language
remained nothing but a strange incantation, a song sung
during a wedding ceremony, a childhood rhyme they
repeated, not knowing its meaning, while playing games

like gonggi or ttangttameokgi. The truth was they thought the old language was ridiculous and pathetic. They did not let this show on the outside. Most of them behaved like they still respected the shaman and did their best not to slight her. But even the shaman did not know that, privately, they treated her with contempt. Almost all the major and minor matters of the tribe were, in fact, handled by their periodically elected chief; the authority held by the shaman was a mere formality. The chief was almost always a man and someone who was proficient in the official language. He procured all the goods the tribe needed, liaised with the government or welfare authorities and represented the tribe to outsiders. When someone got sick or hurt, people immediately called a doctor and borrowed a motorcycle or car from a rich family to take the patient to a nearby hospital. If the shaman stepped in and offered to treat the patient with medicinal powders she had ground up herself, or salves she had made by boiling animal bones and plant roots, people failed to hide their annoyance at having to humour the old woman's silliness.

Sometimes they didn't even bother to humour her. Like when she tried to involve herself with the children's education. The shaman wanted to teach the tribe's children many things – such as the old language, traditional hunting techniques and the laws of marriage and succession – but no parent wanted such instruction. All the mothers spoke as one: 'I'm sorry, Honourable Shaman, but those things won't help the children make a living.' 'We cannot, Honourable Shaman. We must send our children to the school in town to receive welfare benefits.' The chief reasoned with the shaman, using more complicated language: 'Madam, the children must learn the official language. They must learn modern science and financial sense. Otherwise our tribe won't survive.' *Modern. Science. Finance.* Those words came at her in a rush, like they were debris from who-knows-where washing toward her in a flood. *College, internet, Hollywood, law firm, immigration policy, sexism, terrorism, vegetarianism . . .* Whenever the old shaman heard such words, she was overcome with dizziness. She had no idea what any of those words meant. Although it seemed that the people who used them did not know what they meant either. The village was made up of just over a hundred households and not a single person had gone to college. No one used the internet on a daily basis either. No one had gone to Hollywood or worked at a law firm, or knew anything for certain about the people immigrating to this country or about how to emigrate to another country. Either way, people still used those words. They were expressions of an intangible sort of hope. Hope that a different life existed somewhere, that the possibility of such a life was open to them too. Because words were for everyone. Because words did not cost money. Because words could be used by anyone in any way. And so words came first, before everything else. Before the object came the name. Before the money came the catalogue listing all the things that could be bought. Before the government benefits came all the pledges and ads. Before the mining jobs came the job postings, before the job postings came the termination notices . . . Information about support groups for minorities, news about a plan to draft indigenous peoples' welfare laws, telephone calls and letters asking them to share their lives through documentaries and books . . . Still, there were some things that did arrive before there were words for them. For instance, disease, alcohol, drugs. And death. They experienced death sooner than the city people did. Ten years ago, there had been an outbreak of a new, unidentified disease in the tribe. The authorities sent medical and research teams to them, but the disease abated only after dozens of lives had been lost. It was only afterward that scientists officially gave the disease a name.

The shaman thought this was all a sort of curse. That this was the wrath of the spirits, that the tribe had brought corruption and collapse upon itself. The shaman did not trust anything about the outside world and hated everything associated with the central government. She believed the tribe should cut ties with the outside world and return to its ancient ways. To a time when words had connected to objects without issue. To a time when life and labour were in sync with one another. To a time when men were like men, women were like women, and children were like children . . . The shaman herself had not witnessed such a time. But the myths and legends said that it had existed.

No one sympathised with the shaman, but at least she had a granddaughter. Whatever anyone said, Rabi was her irrefutable heir, the one who would preserve the tribe's traditions and memories. And so the shaman stubbornly taught Rabi the way the tribespeople had been taught in the olden days. No matter how much Rabi defied her. No matter how thoroughly Rabi appeared to prove that myth could no longer explain the world, that magic could no longer form the foundation of human lives.

I do not agree with either side. I only watch, and remember. My memory is inherited through my physical self. Humans pass on their wisdom through media such as stories, writing and drawings, but I, we, remember solely through evolution. Because of this, our remembering is slow, but it is complete.

Rabi grew up under her grandmother's thumb until she was fifteen. During most of that time, she prayed for her grandmother's death.

Rabi could not stand her grandmother's style of parenting. Grandmother forbade her from using the official language. She taught Rabi the old language that no one used but herself, and if she heard Rabi's lips stammer out any words in the official language that she'd picked up from the neighbours, she gave Rabi hell. Rabi wasn't allowed to go to school like the other children. Her only teacher was Grandmother and her school was a two-room house in the remotest part of the village, its backyard, and the forest and pond that lay beyond. It was here that Rabi learned the old stories and songs, the superstitions and folk remedies. The way to dance in clothing of woven raffia fibre with her face painted in horrible colours. The way to mash fruits and char roots and extract oils. The way to harvest the heart of a palm tree and add powdered grains to make porridge. The way to take the chickens and pheasants that Grandmother raised in the backyard and cook meals she was sick and tired of making and sick and tired of eating. The things girls shouldn't do, the things she shouldn't do to men or grown-ups or foreigners, the things she shouldn't do on a full moon, the things she shouldn't do when she was menstruating . . . The food she shouldn't eat, the songs she shouldn't sing, the things she shouldn't show interest in no matter the reason . . . The things that were forbidden altogether. Rabi thought she might suffocate to death from all that was forbidden to her. She fought not to die. But Grandmother condemned Rabi's behaviour and said that she was being wicked. That her mind was full of deceit just like her father's, so no wonder she never listened. How was she ever going to be the next shaman with the way she was acting? Even then, though, Grandmother insisted that, some way or another, Rabi should be her successor. Likewise, there were many times Grandmother said things that did not make logical sense. Rabi could not understand her, so she questioned her. Then Grandmother said Rabi was being stupid just like her mother. If Rabi still did not obey, Grandmother beat her.

Rabi was beaten constantly. If she broke any of Grandmother's rules, she was punished without fail. Her cheeks were slapped. She was caned, clubbed, and hit with a stool. Over time, the assaults increased in both frequency and intensity. The taller she grew and the sturdier her bones became – at the same time, the greyer Grandmother's hair turned, the deeper her wrinkles grew, the more crookedly her torso bent – the more Grandmother struck Rabi on impulse. If Rabi picked Grandmother's favourite dragon fruit from the garden and served it to her, she was hit for wasting the precious fruit that was being saved for an important visitor; if she left the dragon fruit untouched, she was hit for not picking it before it rotted away. At some point, Rabi stopped knowing why she was being hit – or perhaps there had never been a reason in the first place. Rabi stopped rebelling at age nine. She stopped crying and apologising at age eleven.

'I'm doing this to protect you,' Rabi's grandmother said one day. 'The world will hurt you. One mistake and you'll end up like your mother.'

Grandmother repeated this constantly. But Rabi had thought that her mother had died giving birth to her. Some might have said that her mother's untimely death was *because* of her. But, strangely, Grandmother only ever blamed 'the world'. Grandmother said that Rabi's mother had died because when Rabi's mother was a girl she'd met a man from a city far away and the man had deceived her. Recklessly, she had given her body over to him. She had climbed into his huge, gleaming car and run off with him, and eventually she had gotten with his child. That's why she died. Grandmother never once referred to Rabi's father as 'your father'. He was always 'that man' or 'that bastard'. There was not one peep from her about why precisely he was bad, why he'd left, what had happened, whether he was alive or dead, and, if he was alive, what he was doing and where.

Rabi imagined vaguely that her father might have been a tourist visiting the village. The village was not a popular tourist destination, nor was there really much to look at, but quite a few people did make their way there, all the way to the hinterlands. The young people of the tribe who were contracted by travel agencies showed tourist groups around the forest or took them rafting in the gentle stream. Girls set up stalls along the route the tourists took and at the village market, to sell the crafts they had made. Things like masks, feather earrings, spears and bamboo bowls. Grandmother always clicked her tongue and criticised them for being shoddy and inauthentic, fake crafts made to appeal to the tastes of the outsiders. Either way, Rabi had no interest in these crafts; she was interested in the tourists themselves. Those people with hair and eyes and skin colours, face structures and clothing itself that were so different from hers. Those people who laughed in a different manner, spoke in a different voice and moved differently from anyone else in the village. They brought life to the village. They were different from the people of the tribe who had lost themselves to deep-seated despair, a habitual sense of shame and alcoholism with no chance of recovery. In Rabi's eyes, the outsiders actually looked alive. They were the ones who looked like they were truly living a life.

Tourists were not the only outsiders who visited the village. Sometimes there were missionaries or outreach volunteers sent from the local government. They brought vitality back to the village in other ways, in the form of medical supplies, colourful clothing and shoes and hats, foods and snacks the tribespeople had never seen before, books and magazines, and sometimes machines and tools and household goods. In Rabi's eyes, the outsiders were all-powerful and benevolent beings. They always spoke in a gentle voice and bestowed wonderful gifts on the tribe without expecting anything in return. Rabi was deeply moved by the kindness she received from them – a kindness that she had never received from anyone else – and even wondered if they might be able to help her. But their kindness, like the scent of the soap wafting from their bodies, was quickly lost to the breeze.

Instead, one by one, Rabi collected the baubles the outsiders had brought for them. A pair of glasses without lenses, a fashion magazine in a language she could not read, a tin box that had once held caramels, a twenty-four-colour pack of paper and a blue minidress. Worried that her grandmother might find her treasures if she left them at home, Rabi buried them all in the earth at the edge of the forest.

Ever since she was a little girl, Rabi had constantly traversed the distance from her backyard to the nearby forest and knew the place like the back of her hand. She knew precisely which tree grew where, which trail led where. My individual plants, which looked identical to some people, she could tell apart easily. And so, she found an exceptionally dense bush of mine and after digging a shallow hole under it she packed her treasures neatly into a paper box, placed it into the hole and covered it with dirt. On top she scattered some leaves and branches so her hiding spot would not stand out.

Rabi was twelve years old at the time. She came to visit me often after that and did many more secret things in my presence. Many more. Her whole life, Rabi shared those secrets with no one except us.

It was not that Rabi favoured us. In fact, it was likely the opposite. She was sick and tired of everything native to the place where she had been born and raised. She had nowhere else to go except to our side. If Rabi mingled with the other girls of the tribe, the shaman pestered her about whether they had taught her to speak the official language, whether they had given her alcohol or cocaine. If Rabi was at home, the shaman watched her every move and brought out the cane at even the smallest transgression. At the very least, if Rabi was in the forest, the shaman thought she was studying medicinal herbs and felt more at ease. And so, by and large, Rabi's only choice was to flee to the forest and spend her time here. Many a day she endured the hunger in her belly because she could not stand to return home and instead lingered by our side, subsisting on berries and mushrooms. Many a day she lay beside us crying or sat beside us spitting curse words. Many a day she came to our side with a basket or a rake in hand while on an errand for her grandmother and whiled away her time, singing the songs her grandmother had taught her with lyrics she had made up. There was nothing else Rabi could do. At least, back then.

Rabi's tribe refers to me as the purple bean plant. The name comes from the vivid purple of my seed hull and its white eye. My leaves are like bird feathers and my flowers a soft lavender. My stem stretches into vines that entwine themselves around various supports. I thrive regardless of my environment. With my sturdy roots I grasp the earth, push past the plants around me and grow in a sprawl.

There is a poison in my purple seeds. It is a weapon devised by our ancestors to protect our offspring from enemies. In the language of humans, it is a weapon intrinsic to our lineage. I, too, armed my tender body with this weapon when I was a sprout. Many animals, humans included, knew full well my family's reputation and mostly kept their distance from me. My poison can permeate your cells and block protein synthesis. If you eat one of my children, you will first start to vomit and have diarrhoea. Then you will become dehydrated, your blood pressure will fall, and you will start having hallucinations and seizures. Within three days, your essential organs will fail entirely and you will die. To date, no antidote has been found.

The old shaman warned Rabi about me over and over. Not only must she never eat one of my seeds, but even touching me was dangerous. The shaman knew how to neutralise my poison but it was still too dangerous a technique to teach young Rabi. It was the same sacred technique used during the shaman initiation ceremony. And so, until she could perform that technique, the shaman insisted that Rabi was not to go near me. But Rabi thought this was just the shaman's superstition, or one of the many things the shaman had declared forbidden to keep her tied down, or perhaps both. Rabi wanted to break all the rules forbidding her from doing things. She wanted to spit brazenly on the faith the shaman so foolishly clung to. The easiest way for her to do this was by handling me however she liked, heedless of her grandmother's words.

And so Rabi spent her time extracting my seeds from their pods and making mischief. One by one, with the tips of her fingers, she popped out my seeds and flung them at random into the grass as if she were tearing off someone's fingernails, imagining my seeds to be the fingernails of the people she hated. Usually this was her grandmother. Rabi extracted my seeds even before they were ripe and, not satisfied with merely flinging them aside, she would grind them into the dirt with a rock. That activity was, in fact, very dangerous. If the strong purple hull of my seeds were to crack or break, the toxic substance within would ooze out; and the merest touch of it upon naked skin was enough to poison someone.

It was not ignorance of the truth that made Rabi reckless. When she was in the forest, she watched the birds. She saw they were completely unaffected by eating my seeds; she knew they did not digest the hulls, but rather passed them as waste. Rabi marvelled at this. She was curious about my friendly relationship with the birds. That is why, after crushing my seeds within the folds of a towel, she smeared the toxic parts of my children onto the surface of a boulder or stirred them into a puddle of rainwater. The birds and other small animals that consumed the poison died one by one. Rabi was delighted to discover the carcasses of wild grouse, shearwaters and parrots.

If Rabi tired of this, she had another way of entertaining herself with me. Out of all the various parts of all the various plants growing here, my deep purple seeds, which were hard and smooth like beads, looked especially artificial. Rabi liked to pretend my seeds were jewels behind the glass windows of a department store in the city, or earrings hanging off the lobes of a famous actress. Every once in a while, if she got bored playing with the secret treasures she had buried and then dug up from under me, she added my seeds into the mix. For instance, she lined up my seeds along the belt of the blue minidress, or she wrapped my seeds in the coloured paper like they were candy and placed them in the caramel tin, or she strung my seeds on a thread and wore them around her neck, put on the glasses and gazed at her reflection in the pond.

Thanks to Rabi's activities, my seeds were able to spread and sprout ever further without going through a bird's digestive system. By the time my sprout grew into a small thicket, Rabi had grown one year older. Towering taller than she had the year before, Rabi surveyed my vines and leaves with an indifferent expression, then used her hands to dig them up once more.

Little by little, Rabi's breasts began to swell and her rear began to round. At age thirteen she started her monthly cycles. The old shaman took Rabi's maturing into a woman as a sign of danger. She thought that someday one of those foreigners who were full of curiosity, or those itinerants who worked in the nearby uranium mines, gaunt with monotony and exhaustion, or those public officials who came to confirm the tribe's bleak prospects and poverty – one of them would rape Rabi. She fretted constantly that the inherent evil of Rabi's temperament would corrupt them.

To set the old shaman's mind at ease, the tribespeople helped to supervise Rabi, but amongst themselves they snickered that she was worried for nothing. No man would ever want to rape a girl as ugly as Rabi. To them, this was all the more reason to keep Rabi hidden from the eyes of outsiders. With her wide, flat face and pockmarked skin, her eyes like buttonholes and her huge, lumbering frame that was covered in bruises, Rabi's appearance was nothing to be proud of. The tribespeople did not want to disappoint the outsiders – those people who saw their fake crafts, their routine songs and dances that were simple enough to perform for television cameras, and praised them as 'mysterious' and 'beautiful' – by bringing the hideous appearance of their shaman's one and only granddaughter to light. It was best to keep that a secret.

'The shaman-to-be cannot come into contact with outsiders until she officially takes her place as shaman. That is our way,' the chief explained with the gravest of expressions.

Rabi thought she would die well before she became either an adult or the next shaman. She thought it more realistic that she would die from her grandmother's beatings than from any harm caused by an outsider man. Grandmother would live on forever and she would most definitely die, tomorrow if not today. This 'today' and 'tomorrow' continued day after day. Every night, Rabi thought of her father. Her father, whose name she didn't even know, whom her grandmother badmouthed every day. Was he going about his life in that other world out there? Did he ever spare a thought for his daughter?

Did he ever wonder how she was doing? Who knew, someday her father might come looking for her, driving his huge, gleaming car from the other world. Whenever Rabi imagined this, her terror subsided a little; then she promptly hated herself for thinking such wicked, foolish thoughts. Sometimes, in her dreams, Grandmother beat her until her bones broke for sharing a toothy grin with her father. But dream-Rabi did not stop smiling, even as she was being beaten.

When Rabi was around sixteen, she stopped playing with my seeds. She grew up too soon, as the native children were wont to do; at her age, she had already learned too much and had lost her ability to imbue my seeds with her imagination. She learned that she was not the first girl to want to drape my beads on her body, nor would she be the last. She learned that her grandmother, and her grandmother's grandmother, and her grandmother's grandmother too, had carried out the ritual of making necklaces and hair ornaments from my beads. She learned that ornaments made from my beads had once symbolised the dignity and solemnity of the shaman. She learned that, decades ago, white women had been fanatic about my beauty too. And she learned that there'd once been a time when the girls of the tribe, who were making purple rosaries out of my beads for those white women to pray with, died en masse because of my poison. After she learned those things, Rabi gradually disappeared and grew distant from me.

Around the same time, Rabi also stopped playing house

with the small toys the outreach volunteers had brought. As memories of their magical kindness and goodwill toward her faded, it became abundantly clear that those objects were not any kind of incredible treasure. They did not save her. They did not heal her wounds. Just as she did not believe in the incantations of a shaman, she stopped believing in the magic of those objects. Thus Rabi abandoned the treasures of her childhood in the dirt and never came for them again.

I wrapped my roots around those objects. My hyphae, which reached far and wide below the earth, entangled them within their net. I watched Rabi's treasures slowly disintegrate. Watched as the enzyme continuously secreted by my mycelium broke down the glasses and the magazine and the tin case and the coloured paper and the dress.

I lived till the day Rabi's possessions had been eaten through by microorganisms, until they had gradually turned to rust and could no longer be distinguished from dirt. That happened many, many years in the future, after Rabi and Rabi's grandmother and Rabi's tribespeople had all died and their corpses and belongings and homes had all rotted away.

When Rabi was eighteen, her grandmother died. Three elders around the same age as her grandmother all passed away one year apart from each other, and her grandmother was the last of them. The old shaman had gone to town to get groceries when a truck hit her at a four-lane intersection and she breathed her last. The truck driver was at fault for going too fast, but the shaman was largely at fault too, for suddenly running out into the road where there wasn't a crosswalk. After checking the black box and CCTV recordings, the police said it looked like suicide or erratic behaviour caused by senility. The tribespeople were furious. Their shaman, who had always been so full of vitality, whose gaze had always been so clear and sharp – their elder who had never once touched alcohol or drugs of any kind – it was unfathomable that she should die by suicide. On top of that, the shamans of their tribe knew nothing of senility. Keeping their icy-cold wits about them, remaining trim and tidy in their bearing until their last breath, that was the essence of being a shaman. That was their qualification, their proof, their privilege of being a shaman. Confronted with a death the likes of which had never happened, the tribespeople, even as they came to question their belief in the godliness of their shaman, realised said belief was still deeply rooted in their lives. And they realised that as soon as that belief was recognised, it was in danger of being uprooted. That was a frightening prospect. Thus they sowed doubt, saying that the police were lying to them by claiming it was suicide or senility, either because they thought little of the tribe or because they were covering for the driver. They got on their motorcycles and staged protests. The chief, along with other men who were knowledgeable about the world, consulted with lawyers and insurance agents. Together, they wrote up all sorts of documents, argued over the phone, raged in despair, went to the driver's home to unleash their anger on him, sent anonymous letters to the media claiming discrimination, and thus combined forces to rake in as much money as possible. The newspapers briefly reported on the death as a freak accident that happened once in a while to the native peoples of the region.

Arguments broke out amongst the tribespeople over how the hard-won compensation from the accident should be managed and distributed. As a result, two families within the tribe grew to detest each other and the entirety of the money was wasted away. By that point, the surge of fear they had all once felt was forgotten.

Rabi did not think her grandmother's death was a suicide. Nor did she think it was an accident. Rabi believed *she* had killed her grandmother. She had prayed over and over and over to the spirits to kill her grandmother and, through some means known only to the spirits themselves, the curse had finally taken form. Rabi had never believed in magic, but she couldn't help but think of it in that moment.

The funeral was held. Rabi inherited a portion of the compensation from the accident, as well as her grandmother's house and memorabilia. As natural as breathing, she became the next shaman. In the past, there would have been a ceremony for Rabi to accept the divine gift that was her birthright. The chief would have invited all the neighbouring relatives and, before them, Rabi would have drunk the brew that neutralised my poison and worn a necklace and hair ornament woven through with my seeds, and then, amidst the singing and dancing of the tribe's youth, she would have ascended with confidence to the role of shaman. But now there was no one who remembered this ceremony. Grandmother died before she could oversee the ritual to make Rabi a shaman; and Rabi, although she had been taught what a shaman needed to know, had *not* been taught the ritual to become one. And so Rabi was left behind – with a two-room house in the remotest part of the village, with the chickens and pheasants that Grandmother had raised in the backyard, with Grandmother's favourite dragon fruit, with the old stories and songs, with the superstitions and folk remedies, with the countless old taboos.

Rabi thought everything would finally be over once her grandmother died. That all taboos would disappear and freedom would unfurl before her. But even after Grandmother's death, there wasn't much Rabi could do. She didn't suddenly become fluent in the official language, nor did her face suddenly become pretty or her skin smooth. Because of this, she couldn't get a job, or get married, or even sell her body. Grandmother had supported herself on the funds she'd received from the government as an ethnic minority elder, but Rabi was young and healthy and a full adult – albeit only just turned eighteen – so she was ineligible to receive such funds. If she wanted to survive, she needed to work. She needed to do something – anything at all.

For while, Rabi found herself helping the other women of the tribe make crafts to sell to tourists, taking on mending work, looking after Grandmother's chickens and pheasants and brewing dragon fruit liquor. In the evenings, she studied the official language. On the weekends, she walked to the village market and set up her stall with eggs, poultry and dragon fruit liquor. Seeing Rabi sell next to nothing, the other merchants took pity on her and traded her a bar of soap or a pack of batteries for some eggs. On the days she sold and traded nothing, during her long trudge back home she sometimes collapsed onto the dirt, sobbing. It was a two-hour walk from the market to her house. Her legs hurt and her feet bled. No matter how much she mended her shoes, they quickly came apart. She needed money for new shoes. No, she needed money for a motorcycle. Right as she came to realise this fact, with a kind of desperation Rabi also realised the accident compensation amount she had received from the chief had been next to nothing.

But she couldn't complain at this point. She didn't want to either. She didn't want to fight to get a little more money from her grandmother's death. What she wanted was the four-wheel-drive car and the motorcycle the chief had at his house. What she wanted was the generator, the refrigerator, the flush toilet he had at his house. The chief's son was the foreman of the uranium mines; it was up to him who could and couldn't work there. All the young men wanted to be friends with him. All the young women wanted to be close with his wife, while secretly wishing to be his mistress. Rabi did not want any of that. She just wanted a motorcycle. But she didn't think she would ever be able to get one, even if she worked every single day of her life.

At night, Rabi drank alcohol. She drank, played cards with the tourists, and spent the night with one of their men. She drank again, then spent the night with a different man. Then she drank again, then spent the night with yet another man. Sometimes a man beat her because she was ugly. Sometimes, while the man slept, she stole the money in his pocket and fled. Sometimes she wandered the forest, completely intoxicated, until she blacked out before me, after which she woke early in the evening, not remembering anything. When Rabi was drunk, she completely forgot the official language. Not a single person understood her drunken ramblings. Even in this state of dissolution, her grandmother's fears never once came true. Rabi was diligent about contraception and the men did not want children with her. No middle-aged male tourist ever came looking for her in his huge, gleaming car. Neither did Rabi ever flash her teeth or giggle at a man. None of it happened.

The morning Rabi turned twenty, as she trod the path to the market to sell her eggs and dragon fruit liquor, her beaded bracelets and feather earrings, she caught up with a group of children on their way to school. Not knowing that Rabi was behind them, they chattered away:

'Shaman? How's that being a shaman? I've never seen her do any kind of magic. All she does is drink and have sex and say weird crap all the time.'

'My ma says she acts like that 'cause she's got a white man's blood in her. So it's like she's not even really part of the tribe.'

'No way.'

'It's true. I'm not kidding. That's what my ma says.'

'Then shouldn't she *not* be the shaman? If she's got white-person blood in her, she should go to church.'

'No, my ma says all shamans are crazy. Like, only crazy women become one.'

Rabi understood then why her grandmother had died. Rabi hadn't killed her. Her grandmother had died from her own fear. She had always been chased by fear.

Rabi suddenly felt very old. All the elders who could

understand her speech had died and left her on this earth completely alone, and now Rabi felt like she had aged several thousands of years in a split second. She felt that she was speaking to her mother, her mother's mother, and her mother's mother's mother. She felt the memories that no one remembered slowly surging through her. Like quicksand. Like a tidal wave. Like time.

My ancestors were born on this planet ninety million years ago. Back when the earth was warmer than it is now. The air was humid, the oceans wide and tranquil, and rivers of hot golden liquid oozed from the ground. Our ancestors enjoyed the fertility of this world that was like one large hothouse and proliferated rapidly. Back then, the land was our kingdom. From under the skies of the equator to the distant regions of the North Pole, we stained every corner of the earth green. As our various languages rode the wind, coursing from place to place without rest, the animals who understood our language came to partake of our nectar and fruit. We fed them and fed on them in turns. That era lasted a long time. It was only until much, much later that the human species emerged and called us 'plants'.

Some men came to learn about us. They were researchers.

When the group of researchers showed up at the village and introduced themselves, the tribespeople were wary. They weren't sure what the researchers' purpose was nor what the researchers were looking to get from them. The tourists wanted to buy fun. The television reporters wanted to buy views. But the researchers' desires were unclear.

'We came because we want to hear stories from your past.'

One of the scholars – a man with an overly friendly smile and an overly loud voice – spoke in front of all the people gathered at the chief's house. He said he was an anthropologist.

'We came because we want to know about your traditions and about the plants here. That's all.'

The chief was a clever man. Rather than blindly dismiss these foreigners who had come from a far-away place, he decided to treat this as an opportunity that might benefit the tribespeople in some way.

He gestured toward Rabi and said in a polite manner, 'Our shaman here is well versed in this matter. She is the embodiment of our tradition. But I am not sure whether she would impart such knowledge to an outsider . . .'

As the chief trailed off, his son nodded and chimed in: 'And besides, none of us, including our shaman, has time to be idle. We all need to work.'

But the researchers didn't seem to have heard them. They were staring at Rabi in surprise. They couldn't have guessed that a young woman like Rabi would have command of a minority language on the brink of extinction.

'My understanding was that the shaman of this tribe was quite elderly,' another one of the researchers said dubiously. He said he was a botanist.

The tribespeople exchanged looks and shook their heads.

'She passed away several years ago.'

The anthropologist let out a cry of distress and suddenly

clasped Rabi's hand in his own. 'I beg your pardon. May she rest in peace.'

The anthropologist stared at Rabi like he would at a rare mineral or a priceless relic. He didn't appear to particularly care whether or not the dead shaman was resting in peace. In response to Rabi's bewildered silence, he began explaining to her with great enthusiasm the subject of his research.

'You have no idea how important your language, your knowledge, is to us. I assure you, it is. Because it contains the entirety of the wisdom and the perspectives of the people who have inhabited this region for hundreds of thousands of years. No one knows what effect that knowledge will have on all of humanity. You may have information about new animals that we haven't yet discovered, or the beginnings of a cure for an incurable disease, or the secret we need to survive a calamity that will befall the earth . . . Your expression says you don't believe me. But in truth, much of what we know has been revealed in this way. You don't know how helpful you will be to us. When I think of you and your language disappearing without anyone knowing . . .'

His rapid, long-winded explanation in the official tongue continued until he saw Rabi's blank expression. He lowered his voice.

'Don't feel pressured. Just think of it as sharing your stories with us. We want to hear what you know about plants. What plants your tribe eats, what you use for medicine, what you use as clothing. And plants you've used for any other purpose besides . . . You only need to tell us to the best of your ability.'

Rabi hesitated. 'But what if none of it is any use to humanity?'

The anthropologist paused. 'Well, the diversity of knowledge in and of itself is worthy of . . .'

The botanist cut him off. 'You don't need to worry about that. We're not here for anything that grand. We just want to live here for a few months with all of you. We'll do our best not to get in your way. We'll help you with your work too. And, every now and then, if you shared some of your old stories with us, we'd of course be grateful. We will offer some of our own gifts too, as an expression of thanks. Will that be all right?'

The botanist's words were much easier to understand. As soon as the word 'gift' was mentioned, the tribespeople's faces brightened with understanding. They turned their gaze to Rabi. Rabi recoiled in surprise. Their entire attention fixed on her like it never had before, with eyes full of expectation. Or, rather, something closer to hunger.

Rabi didn't even have the chance to respond. Starting with the chief, the adults of the tribe each began saying something, their tone one of utmost gravity.

'If you follow our traditions and lifestyle, then I don't see why not.'

'This opportunity to inform the world of our magnificent traditions will please our late shaman as well.'

'Shaman Rabi here inherited everything of her grandmother's wisdom and nature. Indeed, her training was quite severe. Do ask our honourable shaman whatever questions you may have about our plants. There is nothing she won't know.'

Rabi said nothing, looking sideways at the anthropologist. She was actually thinking of something else. She was thinking that this was the first time a man had looked at her ugly face with such passion.

*Long ago, there was an old woman. One night, the old woman dreamed the moon spoke to her: 'On the night of the full moon, go to the pond in the forest and you will find a child. Take the child and raise her as your own.' Four nights later, when the moon was in the sky, the old woman went to the pond. There in the grass, on the edge of the pond, was a baby crying. It was a baby girl. The old woman took the baby home, gave her the name Moon Child, and devoted herself to raising the girl as her own daughter.*

*Moon Child grew into a sweet and pretty girl in no time. Except for one strange ability. Whenever Moon Child would spit, her saliva turned into all sorts of treasures. Things like plates, coral, amber, combs, bells and mirrors. Thanks to those items, the old woman quickly became rich.*

*The villagers were suspicious of where and how the old woman kept getting her hands on these precious goods. The men among them were determined to get to the bottom of the old woman's secret, so when the woman was out selling her treasures, the men seized the opportunity to go to her house. Inside the house, Moon Child was spitting and turning her saliva into pearls. When the men surrounded Moon Child and demanded her pearls, she handed them out to everyone there.*

*After that day, whenever the old woman was absent from her home, the men went to receive treasures from Moon Child.*

*They meant to keep this a secret amongst themselves, but rumours began to fly. More and more people came looking for Moon Child as the days went by. As the days went by, they made more demands and Moon Child fulfilled all of them. She made them crystals, vases, hand fans, incense burners and silks.*

*On the ninth day of this, the people of the village came together and decided that Moon Child could not be left to carry on as she had. They no longer viewed the girl's ability to conjure at will an endless supply of precious, valuable goods with wonder; now, they were full of rage and envy and fear.*

*On the night of the crescent moon, one of the men crept into Moon Child's home and strangled her to death. He left her body there and fled into the dark.*

*The old woman, sobbing in anguish upon discovering her daughter's corpse, then divided the body into several pieces and buried them in the earth. From the pieces of Moon Child's body grew plants that the world had never seen. From her head grew a coconut tree; from her breasts, a sago palm. From her rear came sweet potato; from her genitals, dragon fruit; from her feet, taro. And from her hand, I grew.*

*Those who witnessed this came together to harvest these crops. And this became the very first farm.*

It was not easy for the anthropologist to understand Rabi's tale. Her use of the official language was awkward and there was no one who could translate her words either. The anthropologist had no choice but to learn the old language to a certain extent. He managed to obtain from somewhere tape recordings and a vocabulary book created by a researcher who had studied the language of a neighbouring tribe – Rabi didn't even know such things existed – and used them as a foundation for learning Rabi's language.

Rabi had never imagined the day would come when she would be teaching anyone, let alone a foreign man, her ancient language. She worried if she'd be a good teacher, but the anthropologist did not seem concerned. For the most part, he was content to believe that he understood, in his own way, most of what Rabi was saying.

Rabi occupied her days telling the foreigners old stories and teaching them the old language. Sometimes she sang them ancient songs or showed them ancient magic. She demonstrated the way to dance in clothing of woven raffia fibre, her face painted in horrible colours. The way to mash fruits and char roots and extract oils. The way to harvest the heart of a palm tree and add powdered grains to make porridge. The way to cook chickens and pheasants into meals she was sick and tired of making and sick and tired of eating. The anthropologist would combine his imperfect command of the old language with Rabi's imperfect command of the official language to understand what she was saying, and then discuss further with the botanist and his other colleagues in the official language.

The process took much time and effort and required the labour of many. Women and men alike rolled up their sleeves to help with jobs like kindling the fire, stirring the saucepan, grinding palm flour and sewing. Even people who were busy going to and from work or school poked their heads in, wanting to lend a hand. Everyone wanted to tell the researchers some piece of lore they'd heard from their mother or grandmother or mother's grandmother, lore that they hadn't even known they remembered. Every once in a while their stories clashed and they squabbled, but it never turned into a full-fledged fight. The researchers said it didn't matter who was right and that they didn't have to worry. For the first time in a long while, life returned to the tribe. Some of the elders shed tears anew at the memory of Rabi's grandmother; some of the youth even came forward and apologised for speaking ill of Rabi.

Rabi found all of these changes confusing. The tribe suddenly looked happy. And it wasn't just because of the researchers' gifts – that is, it wasn't because of the money. Of course, the money was important too, but it wasn't everything. They were happy they had something to do, happy they were doing it together, and happy because they saw this as something they were doing for themselves, not for anyone else. Indeed, the researchers made them feel like they were doing this work for no one else but themselves. This was different from the tourists or television report-ers. The researchers did not shun or look down their noses at Rabi or Rabi's tribe. They cooked and ate alongside the tribe, helped them sweep and repair their homes, make furniture and slaughter livestock. In the evenings they played the guitar and sang. In the mornings they strolled through the forest or fields, looking around at the plants and animals, taking photos or collecting samples. They had brought a number of strange and complicated devices with them; while using the chief's electric generator to charge their devices, they allowed others to touch them. Things like laptops, smartphones, cameras and microscopes. Sometimes they cried. Sometimes they talked about their hometowns. They drank coffee out of their tumblers and debated amongst themselves. Or they listened to the satellite radio. Or they kicked around a ball with the men of the tribe in an open area. The smell that rose from their bodies, both when they worked and when they played ball, was the same smell that rose from the bodies of the tribespeople. The smell of dirt and grass and sweat.

The tribespeople liked them and had faith in them. But Rabi did not trust them at all; she could not figure out what on earth they wanted. They did not seem particularly moved by Rabi's stories or songs or dance. While they did note down in earnest all of the knowledge she imparted to them, there was no way to know what that earnestness was actually for. Once, when one of the researchers was bitten by a leech, Rabi thought she ought to prepare some medicine for him and stopped by the researchers' residence. But they looked like they had no idea why Rabi would be there. It was a brief moment, but that was when Rabi realised they didn't believe in her magic at all. They didn't expect to benefit personally from her healing techniques or blessings or wisdom, nor did they even feel the need to. And yet they were saying they'd give Rabi and her tribe money in exchange for their knowledge. Was it okay to accept that money? She couldn't shake off the feeling that the tribe was being deceived.

As always, it was the chief's job to receive the money from the researchers and distribute it. Rabi trusted the chief just as little as she trusted the researchers. When the chief declared that the tribe's life and very future would change because of their 'collaboration' with the researchers,

the tribespeople were inspired – but whatever the researchers planned to do here, Rabi didn't think her house would
get bigger, or that she would get a refrigerator or flush toilet
installed or a motorcycle to ride. The researchers were not
going to lay down asphalt roads, or establish a fair trade
contract, or build a hospital either.

In particular, the anthropologist – the researcher with
whom she interacted the most often – frightened Rabi.
Unlike many of the other researchers, who were con-
sistently mild-mannered and thus hard to decipher, the
anthropologist was prone to wild mood swings because he
couldn't figure her out. He was so easily touched by the
smallest kindness Rabi showed him, yet would become des-
pondent because of one throwaway comment. He clung
tightly to his research; his bloodshot eyes were always
scouring his laptop or scanning through his books and
papers. There was always an anxiousness in his expression, as if he were being chased by something. Sometimes,
very rarely, if he had trouble understanding Rabi, he got
irritated.

'What are you even talking about? What's this about a
spirit?'

'For the love of god, say something that makes sense.'

One time, when he was learning the old tribal language,
he picked a quarrel with Rabi because he couldn't understand something. That something was about a plant. Me,
to be exact.

'You're saying that in your language the phrase "to go
senile" is "a purple bean vomits"? Why? Why is that the
expression? You don't know? You're telling me a shaman

like you knows nothing about this? Besides, wouldn't the purple bean *be vomited,* not be the thing that vomits? It doesn't make sense grammatically. Something's off . . .'

When the anthropologist lashed out like this, Rabi shrank from him. The truth was Rabi wasn't a proper shaman. She was a pseudo-shaman who hadn't even gone through the initiation ceremony. A fake shaman with the blood of a foreigner. She was constantly on edge. Did this man doubt her authenticity? Could he spot her weakness? Did he consider her unqualified and look down on her? But then the next day the anthropologist would once again behold her with wonder in his eyes, just as he had the first day he saw her, saying, 'You are the last true shaman of this age.' His words, which implied Rabi was the last shaman and there would be no one to follow in her footsteps, left a foul taste in her mouth. She did not know whether she was supposed to be happy or offended.

Thankfully, though, Rabi wasn't the only one who didn't like the anthropologist very much. She could tell that his occasional outbursts resulted in an air of uneasiness among the other researchers too. He seemed to be on bad terms with the botanist in particular. The botanist was the anthropologist's opposite on many levels. He was taciturn and chilly in his demeanour, and his facial expression rarely varied. The only time he frowned or raised his voice was when he argued with the anthropologist. But they were careful not to let their discord show, so Rabi found it difficult to know why exactly they were at odds.

One day, the anthropologist, who had finished making a record of Rabi's 'Tale of Moon Child', was in the middle of a heated exchange with the botanist in their language. The anthropologist spoke and the botanist snapped back animatedly, to which the anthropologist's voice rose with even more passion. This verbal tussle carried on for a while. It was the first time they had fought in front of Rabi. Not only were they speaking too fast, but their conversation was full of complicated vocabulary – although she did understand some of the words they repeated, like 'Moon Child', 'purple bean' and 'farming'. Rabi had been watching them silently, like she was invisible, when all of a sudden the anthropologist turned to ask her a question.

'Rabi, could you tell us that story again? The one about Moon Child. Which plants did you say grew from Moon Child's body?'

'The Tale of Moon Child' was one of the tribe's oldest legends. And one that Rabi had heard countless times from her grandmother.

Without a moment's hesitation, she replied, 'Coconut tree, sago palm, sweet potato, dragon fruit, taro and purple bean.'

The anthropologist was well versed in this type of folktale. It was one of the common stories passed down across this cultural area to explain the emergence of food crops and the origins of farming practices. When a goddess is buried in the earth, her flesh is reborn as blessed food crops; through the death of the goddess humans evolve the ability to farm for the first time. Some of the details in Rabi's story were different from the versions the anthropologist knew but for the most part they were the same. Moon Child had provided Rabi's tribe with essential fruits like coconut and sago and tubers like sweet potato and taro. With the change in climate and soil quality, they now preferred to work in the uranium mines rather than compete in cultivating palm fruits and taro, but nevertheless the memory of their first agricultural endeavour was passed down in their stories.

One point of interest was the dragon fruit. While dragon fruit was indeed a tropical plant, it wasn't indigenous to the region and, according to the data, neither this tribe nor its neighbours had ever imported and grown it as a key crop. But the fact that dragon fruit appeared in Rabi's Moon Child myth meant that at some point it *had* played an important role. That past may well have influenced the content of the story, resulting in the version Rabi knew.

But what the anthropologist could not understand was the next part. The part about the 'purple bean plant' growing from Moon Child's hands.

According to the botanist, I was not a food crop. A toxic plant like myself could not be more different from the foods that contributed to human survival, like palm fruits and tubers and dragon fruit. Some regions had developed a traditional remedy out of my leaves and oil, but those were places with highly advanced ancient civilisations. The only thing that was certain was the deadliness of the poison in my seeds. Throughout history, animals, including humans, avoided me, knowing that consuming my seeds would lead to death.

Why *I* was mentioned in a story about a goddess granting humans plants that were beneficial to them, the anthropologist could not understand.

The researchers asked Rabi how the tribe made use of the purple beans. She said that it was customary to drink a brew made of them during the shaman's initiation ceremony. When the researchers asked her how that brew was made, her face stiffened and she pressed her lips shut.

When the researchers started to ask about how to neutralise me, Rabi became even more frightened. In her desperation, she told them she could not reveal that because it was a secret. She couldn't come up with any other excuse. Luckily, her plan was effective. The researchers interpreted Rabi's intractability as anger linked to her pride in the tribe, and dropped the matter for the time being. And so Rabi was able to hide from them the fact that she was completely ignorant of the shaman's initiation ceremony.

But the anthropologist did not give up. Sweetly he asked if Rabi could tell him any other stories she knew about me. Sweetness did not suit him but he did make an effort. He pleaded with her to relay any other folktale, proverb, history, application – anything at all – that involved me, even if it was a vague memory or a personal anecdote.

Rabi was at a loss. She hadn't thought about me in years but, because she'd spent so much time with me as a girl, in her own way she *did* know quite a lot. But she didn't think any of it was worth sharing with the researchers. The story of how she'd popped out my seeds, one by one, from their pods and flung them away? That you need to wear gloves when crushing up my seed hulls because it's dangerous? Why birds are unharmed when they eat my seeds? That she'd pretended my seeds were gems and played house?

Rabi may not have known much, but even she knew that such silly, trivial things would be of no use to humanity. What else was there? That, in the past, a shaman would wear a necklace and headband made of my seeds during her initiation ceremony, but that Rabi had never even witnessed such a ceremony, much less undergone one herself? Or perhaps that tragic story of the women of her grandmother's grandmother's generation who made rosaries out of my seeds for white women to pray with and then died because my poison touched their skin?

Rabi said she did not know any more stories. But the anthropologist did not believe her. Suspecting that she was keeping a secret from him, he pretended to give up on the matter for a while and then brought it up again. Rabi was shaken by the anxiety marring his face. She remembered his reproach: *A shaman like you knows nothing about this?* She also remembered the kids badmouthing her: *How's that being a shaman? She's not even really part of the tribe. Only crazy women become shamans.* But at the same time she remembered the anthropologist's praise toward her: *You are the last true shaman of this age.* And she remembered the chief's lip service: *She has inherited everything of our last shaman's knowledge and nature, and is the embodiment of our tradition.* She remembered the tribespeople looking at her with eyes full of anticipation, speaking to her with warm words. The sudden happiness that had filled their lives. And she remembered what it had been like before.

Rabi felt pressured to tell him something. Something that sounded plausible. But Rabi, too, had a sense of what 'plausible' sounded like. She could borrow here and there from the legends and incomplete anecdotes she knew, weave them together, and make up a new story in a flash. That would be easy. So Rabi simply did that. Acting like she couldn't win against the anthropologist, she pretended reluctance and told him about my significance to the tribe's shamans and why the exact way I am used is a secret.

'The seed of the purple bean plant is considered a holy fruit in our tribe. This is because it was a gift to the descendants of Moon Child. That is, to us shamans. You could say it is a privilege and a symbol for us shamans alone.

'So we wear a necklace and a hair ornament woven with the seeds of the purple bean plant during our initiation ceremony. We wear those magenta seeds and show the world we are beautiful, dangerous, powerful beings. The young men of the tribe dance in a circle around us and sing to us, and we take the purple bean seeds that we're holding in our mouths and distribute them among the men. We give more seeds to the men who perform well and fewer seeds to the ones who do not, but everyone gets at least one. How do we hold the seeds in our mouth if they're poisonous? Because we are shamans. And the young men are honouring our special power.

'The maiden who is to be the future shaman chooses the young man who performs the most impressive song and dance. That night, that man must lie with the maiden and make her bleed from her genitals. Before this, the maiden must drink a brew made from the purple beans and defeat the spirits of death, then cleanse her body.

'If the night is spent like this, Moon Child will grant the maiden a special vision of the future. As soon as the girl wakes the following morning, she must tell her dream of Moon Child to the man she lay with the night before. What she tells him must be something that no one has ever heard, that no one will ever again hear.

'The man who hears the dream will then announce to the whole tribe that she has become a true shaman. From that day forward, the maiden will ascend to the position of shaman, and on that joyous occasion everyone will share a delicious feast.'

When the story was finished, Rabi looked over at the anthropologist's face. He looked thrilled. Rabi realised she had told the anthropologist exactly the sort of story he wanted to hear. And she didn't just feel a simple relief; she felt a weight lift off her chest like never before.

If Grandmother were still alive, she would have collapsed in complete and utter fury over the whole situation. If she saw foreign men being invited into the village, saw them eating and sleeping among the people of the tribe. If she knew the tribe's sacred knowledge was being sold to them. If she knew that *fake* knowledge, of all things, was being sold to them. But Grandmother could say nothing now. She was dead. The grim memory of her grandmother that always hovered by Rabi's side receded like fog and the spectre of her past dissipated. A dead person cannot speak. In the face of that truth, Rabi felt better.

It didn't matter whether or not Rabi actually knew the secret about me. No one knew my secret anyway. That secret – the elders who understood what it meant were all dead. So whatever Rabi did, however she used the words of the dead, there was no one to argue with her or get angry with her. There was no one to beat her. They would be silent forever; Rabi would be the only one to speak.

For the first time, Rabi was not afraid of her loneliness. She felt, for the first time, the freedom offered by that loneliness.

The anthropologist and the botanist came looking for me. They inspected me carefully, then uprooted me and took me somewhere. They examined my leaves and seeds. They dissected my body, scrutinised it and analysed it. They tested my toxicity and investigated a standard variety of ways to use my poison.

The anthropologist suspected that I had potential as a powerful and as-yet-undiscovered psychotropic drug. Most importantly, there were numerous clues indicating that I might be a possible cure for Alzheimer's. For him, the biggest clue was that, generation after generation, the shamans of this tribe never went senile. The people believed the shaman to be more put-together than anyone else, that naturally she possessed an intelligent mind. They believed her mind would not falter even as she took her final, dying breath. They espoused this belief not even knowing it was their belief. The fury that they'd felt toward the police for coming to the absurd conclusion that their shaman had gone senile and killed herself was hardly an overreaction. When the anthropologist went to the library in town to look for references, he noted that the tribespeople's public protest of the police's inaction had even made the newspapers.

On top of that, the stories Rabi had told him also

supported his hypothesis. She had more or less implied that generations of shamans, through consuming a medicinal brew made of me, had been granted special mental powers. The vision that they referred to as 'Moon Child's blessing' was likely a side effect of that medicine. But the shamans would not have wanted to reveal this secret that allowed them to enjoy abilities and authority surpassing those of regular people. In order to keep this knowledge contained within their secret religious ceremony, they would have decreed all sorts of restrictions surrounding the purple bean plant . . . For example, only the shaman could wear the purple beans as ornaments; only the shaman could drink the brew; if anyone other than the shaman went near the plant, they'd get hurt . . . Long ago, they would have emerged victorious in the internal struggle for power in this manner; at present, presumably, the knowledge related to the purple bean plant was found in bits and pieces and passed on through the old language's proverbs and myths.

But the botanist was sceptical of the anthropologist's hypothesis. He pointed out that I was quite a common plant and that plenty of research had already been done on me. At best, my seeds contained ingredients that could be used to make laxatives or painkillers, and even if some as-yet-undiscovered psychotropic substance *were* in me, there was little chance it would have any significant impact as a modern-day pharmaceutical. Plus, the poison in my seeds was just a protein. If you applied high enough heat for a certain period of time, my simple protein structure would denature. He stressed that there was no great secret trick to 'neutralising' my poison that only the shamans knew. The botanist criticised his colleague: the reason they had come here on this joint study was to restore and record the indigenous cultural and ecological practices of this land. *Not* to go on an adventure to find some magical wonder drug.

The anthropologist got angry. He accused the botanist of ignoring the validity of anthropological arguments and downplaying the potential of the knowledge being transferred among ethnic minorities. Could the botanist really guarantee that the facts the botanical and pharmaceutical industries had revealed about me were everything? How could a scholar be so arrogant? They ought to know how to respect the knowledge of the indigenous tribes who'd had ties with me for hundreds of thousands of years. They had to learn how to brew the medicine that no one but Rabi still knew how to brew. Once the medicine's effectiveness was verified, Rabi would be given proper public recognition and compensation, and they would help her contribute to the common good . . .

The botanist laughed in disbelief.

'How do you propose to learn about this sacred knowledge that's supposedly being passed down in secret from shaman to shaman? At the end of the day, you're toppling the system they have within the tribe. Is that your way of "respecting" their knowledge? Is that what an anthropologist does? I don't know – I don't think any of the other researchers would support you on that, myself included.'

Seeing the anthropologist's face go blotchy with rage, the botanist lowered his voice a little. Half teasing, he continued with the air of someone consoling his lower-ranking colleague: 'Be honest, aren't you doing all this because you want to get promoted? I understand you feel snubbed by academia because the research you pushed for so long amounted to nothing, but you're going to get in trouble if you rush headlong into things like this. There's a limit to the time and funding we have. We've got to be wise with how we use it.'

At the word 'wise' the anthropologist shut his mouth tight. Hearing his colleague twist his true intentions into something malicious, he thought there was no point in saying anything more. Of course it would be exciting if his hypothesis proved to be definitively correct. It would mean hope for the thousands of Alzheimer's patients all over the world – and it would help his academic reputation. But before they could actually commercialise a new drug, they would need to go through years of animal testing and clinical trials, and that process meant passing the baton to the medical and pharmaceutical industries. At the end of the day, that was a problem for someone else to deal with; there wasn't much the anthropologist could do. Except – he felt something like a desperate obligation toward this. Or perhaps obsession is a better word. An obsession with holding on to everything that seemed to be slipping through his fingers without his knowing. An obsession with rescuing every bit of possibility trapped in the uncharted darkness and releasing it all into the clear light of day.

A girl named Rabi held all of that possibility in her hands. All she needed to do was open her mouth. Then he could test the validity of her information, with a different researcher if need be, and *then* if he felt like it was still not working out he'd give up. In any case, the anthropologist could not just sit back and watch as this girl, right in front of him, stubbornly withheld information that she so obviously knew.

Rabi was standing by the window and listening to the researchers' conversation.

She was still unused to the official language, but her skills had gotten much better through her interactions with the researchers. Straining her ears and listening attentively, she got a decent sense of what the anthropologist and the botanist were arguing about. At least, she could understand enough to know why they were so interested in me.

For a moment Rabi stood lost in thought. Suddenly, she smiled.

That evening, for the first time in many years, Rabi came looking for me. Moving more gracefully than she had when she was a child, she came close to me and dug up my vines and leaves and then popped a few of my ripened seeds from their pod. This time, unlike when she was a child, she examined my seeds with eyes full of interest and curiosity.

Rabi remembered the way she'd crushed and smashed and flung my seeds when she was a child. She remembered the way she'd attached the seeds to the belt of the blue dress and strung them into a necklace that she wore around her neck and looked at her reflection in the pond. She remembered killing small animals with my seeds. Rabi began to play once more with my seeds and the pond water. It was similar to the way she'd played with me when she was younger but also quite different. Now, she was looking for how the animals who consumed my seeds *didn't* die.

Late one night, the anthropologist came looking for Rabi.

When Rabi opened the door, she realised she had been expecting him. The anthropologist strode further into Rabi's rickety old two-room house and seated himself at the dining table. Rabi served him some of the dragon fruit liquor she had brewed herself; he pretended to take a couple of sips and then said, point-blank, 'Tell me the secret. I will do anything.'

Rabi only stared at him.

'After all, you don't have offspring of your own, do you?' he continued resolutely. 'Do you truly think an heir will come forward, willing and able to learn the old language and the wisdom you have? Even if you had a child in the future, will that child truly commit to being a shaman? From what I've heard, you yourself did not want to be a shaman at first.'

Rabi lowered her gaze, saying nothing.

'Wouldn't it be a shame? For all of this to be forgotten? I don't know about you, but I find that heartbreaking. It's such a pity to me. Certainly as a scholar, but even just as a person. That is why I sincerely wish to learn what you know. If I need to be your heir in order to do so, I will. I will go through the ceremony and live the rest of my life as a shaman. I will endure this, even if it means I have to abandon my old life. Your language and your knowledge are more than worth it. What do you think? Do I not qualify? Because I am a man?'

Rabi hesitated. No, she pretended to hesitate. The truth was Rabi did not believe a single word the anthropologist was saying.

To the anthropologist, Rabi's silence felt longer than it was. At last, she began to speak.

'Don't you think, maybe, if I lived a good life . . . that is, if I lived such a good life that people envied me, wouldn't my children want to live like me?' Rabi said with a sad smile. 'In the olden days, the purple bean seeds were a means of displaying the shaman's authority. But in today's world, that's no longer the case. A person's authority is now found in the way they dress, the way they speak, how big their house is, the car they drive. Not in a necklace made out of fruit seeds.'

The anthropologist's expression darkened.

'Whether it's you or someone else, I don't want the next shaman to lead a life as pathetic as the one I lead. I don't want anyone to feel like they are sacrificing themselves to take on the role of shaman. I've had enough of that.'

'Then . . . ?' The anthropologist sounded impatient.

'I need money. I want to buy authority. Something that even the chief won't be able to overlook.'

The anthropologist understood her meaning right away. Disapproval flickered across his face but he quickly hid his expression.

Rabi's request was good for him, in fact. Rather than suffer by her side under the pretence of becoming the next shaman, handing over money was much more convenient. The anthropologist quickly finished his calculations and nodded.

'If you let me know the secret, I can bring you the money right away. You have a bank account, I'm sure? You don't? In that case, I can bring you cash. Except . . . let's keep this between us. Okay? I'll keep your secret, so you don't go telling my colleagues what we're up to either.'

Rabi, of course, did not believe for one second that the anthropologist would keep any secrets.

Early the following morning, the anthropologist told his colleagues he needed to buy something and set out in his car down the forest road. Rabi watched him depart through her window. His car was huge, but did not gleam; it was a shabby black car, so thickly covered in dust that it was closer to a dull grey colour. For the first time, Rabi realised that no car that regularly came and went from this remote neck of the forest would ever sparkle and gleam.

When night fell, the anthropologist returned in his shabby black car and, with a wad of cash in hand, he knocked once more on Rabi's door.

Once Rabi had checked the amount, her teeth flashed in a grin and she told him the story he wanted to hear.

*I have watched the shamans of this tribe for centuries. I have seen the mothers of the shaman family pass on their duties to their daughters and the daughters pass them on to their daughters. I have observed the faces of so many countless daughters resembling, or not resembling, their mothers and grandmothers. I have seen them all, remember them all. So, of course, I remember the day Rabi's grandmother became the shaman like it was yesterday.*

*Of course, the age of the shaman had already come to pass.*

This was not the age of shamans conjuring the sunshine and winds of the dry season and the clouds of the wet season at will. But back then the people of the tribe still fiercely loved their traditions, even as they despaired at their harsh decline. And every man of the tribe, without exception, loved their shaman too. The shaman – that is, Rabi's grandmother – was also named Rabi. Back then she was young and beautiful. Her strong, sleek, brown body radiated warmth and her dark eyes shone with the heat of a charcoal fire while her thick black hair hung to her calves. Her every movement overflowed with vitality and the sound of her brilliant laughter was enough to cleanse the sadness from people's souls. It was no wonder, then, that all the men had given their hearts to Rabi. From the son of the chief to the son of the wealthiest tribesman; from the warrior with the most courage to the hunter who caught the most game, all of them loved Rabi. But in Rabi's heart, there was one man who stood above them all.

The day Rabi became a shaman, she wore a neckpiece woven from beads of gold, coral and my magenta seeds in three loops around her neck. She wore a gold crown in her hair, studded with my seeds and stones of garnet, accented with cinnabar, and she wore a dress adorned with the most fragrant blooms: flamingo flowers, royal poinciana, birds of paradise and orchids. The day Rabi, thus bedecked, watched as the men of the tribe danced and sang in a circle around her, I watched her gaze fix on one man alone. The man was a servant in Rabi's household, an orphan and a cripple who spoke with a stutter.

Limping, the man made a ridiculous attempt at a dance and carefully sang the notes he had taken pains to practise. When his awkward performance ended, Rabi removed some fruit from her mouth. It was dragon fruit pulp studded with black seeds. She had gifted the other men one of my seeds, but to the servant alone she gifted her special fruit of choice. That meant he had been chosen as Rabi's man.

Rabi's mother was angry but she couldn't go against her daughter's decision. No one could halt the sacred ceremony. That night, the servant entered Rabi's room. Rabi had brewed a holy medicine by boiling three hundred of my seeds with thirty of my leaves in water for five hours, then adding a handful of velvet bean roots, a pinch of pepper, a pinch of nutmeg and ten petals of wild passionflower, and boiling for another five hours. Rabi drank the medicine and lay with her man. The two lovers were in bliss. Having kept their love secret until this day, they now lost themselves to their overwhelming joy; and through the night they made love again and again.

But their bliss lasted but a single night. The next day, a messenger and soldiers from the government arrived on their doorstep. A war had broken out and they were drafting all young men to fight. Rabi's mother seized this opportunity and offered up the man Rabi had chosen – the man she loved, the crippled, stuttering servant, the one who had eaten the dragon fruit from her mouth – to the soldiers. Rabi was angry but she couldn't go against her mother's decision. The servant had no parents nor any close blood relatives; he was at his master's disposal at all times. He could not go against the central government either. Their will trumped that of the whole tribe.

The servant left the village before he had the chance to bid Rabi a proper farewell. And Rabi could not tell her lover beforehand about the dream she had dreamed that holy night. The dream that no one had yet heard, that no one now will ever hear.

Rabi waited and waited for the day she would be reunited with her lover. So she would not forget what she wished to tell him, every day, she recounted her dream to the dragon fruit tree in the backyard. The dragon fruit listened to Rabi's tale in silence.

One year passed and then another. The dragon fruit tree diligently bore fruit. Five years passed, thirty years passed. The dragon fruit tree grew tall and strong, and bore the most delicious fruit in the village. Its flesh always smelled and tasted just like the fresh, sweet pulp that Rabi had held gently in her mouth and gifted to her lover. Whenever she ate dragon fruit, Rabi vividly recalled her lover's foolish yet guileless face looking up at her. She took solace in the memory and brewed dragon fruit liquor as she waited for her lover. But her lover did not return. Not even a corpse.

Because the shaman must have an heir, Rabi reluctantly bore a child with a man she did not love at all. As was her duty as shaman, she taught her daughter everything. But her grown daughter, after meeting a bad man, rejected her destiny as shaman and ran away. All too soon after giving birth to the man's child, she died. Rabi did not cry. She had no tears left.

Rabi suspected that she would die before her lover returned. The dream that no one had yet heard was to vanish without ever having been heard, along with Rabi's body. Even the very fact that Rabi had waited until her dying day for her lover *would not remain on this earth. Even if her lover finally returned after all those many years, there would be no one who knew him, no one who loved him, no one who shared his blood; the only one to welcome him would be her dragon fruit tree.*

*Rabi thought long and hard about how she might convey what she wished to her lover. Eventually she decided to take an old tribal legend and weave the origin story of the dragon fruit tree into a part of it. She told this tale to her granddaughter and heir.*

*One week later, Rabi passed away in a mysterious accident. Along with her name, her granddaughter inherited the house with the dragon fruit tree.*

The money Rabi received from the anthropologist was about the same as the total compensation from her grand-mother's death. She had no idea how long that amount of money would last in the city but she took courage in the fact that, at least for the first night, she wouldn't go hungry. Thanks to the anthropologist, her proficiency in the official language had increased significantly; since she had also learned how to speak in a refined manner, with some luck she might even be able to find a job. Perhaps she was being overly optimistic, but she held firm to her self-confidence. In any case, Rabi had definitely earned her own money, with her own skills. The solid proof of that was in her hand.

Rabi was grateful to all the people who made up her current self. Her mother who'd passed down her body. Her grandmother who'd told her stories. Her tribespeople who'd taught her survival skills. The men she had been with who'd shown her the world. Out of them all, she felt the most gratitude to the anthropologist. His suggestion had given Rabi a brilliant idea. Yes, she would go to the city. She would go to the city, save up money, go to college and become a medical doctor. Those men who were anthropologists or botanists or whatever with their fancy doctoral degrees were, embarrassingly, not that smart. If people like that could get their PhDs, Rabi believed she was more than capable. Not to mention, rather than wait for anthropologists or botanists or whoever to unearth and find a use for her knowledge, it would be much faster and more reasonable if Rabi herself found a use for it. She knew about the plants of this region, about the tribespeople of this region, better than anyone. Perhaps even better than her grandmother.

It wouldn't be easy, of course. But it was worth trying. If she successfully became a doctor, she would come back to this village and cure the tribe's diseases and get rid of all the alcohol and drugs. If there was an outbreak of an unidentified disease, she wouldn't wait for a medical team from the city to arrive, she would fight it herself. She would make it so that no woman would die giving birth to a child. She would take care of kids who were like her, who walked with a limp, who always got bruises and nosebleeds, so they would never get hurt again. She could even make it so that kids like her were never born in the first place. She would live in the biggest house in the village, drive the biggest car and take out ice from the biggest freezer and make ice cream for all the children. Every season, she would perform

vaccinations and health check-ups. She would bear responsibility for the life and death, joys and sorrows of all her
people and be regarded, in turn, with both respect and awe.
The daughters who succeeded her would be happy. They
would want to live just like their mother and they would
compete with one another to be named her true heir.

Rabi packed lightly. She wore the sturdiest shoes she
owned and took several additional pairs of shoes and socks.

Before leaving, she looked around the house and tidied
up her things. That's when she discovered a couple of items
she had never seen before in the depths of her grandmother's drawer: a darkly discoloured, worn-looking necklace
and a mouldy headband.

Rabi knew exactly what these items were. She grabbed
them and exited her house. Then she threw them into
the pond in the forest beyond her backyard. In the still-
ness we heard the plop, the sound of the water's surface
breaking.

Early in the morning, before the break of dawn, Rabi left
that place for good.

Five human years passed. The climate changed and
my habitat expanded. North of Rabi's village, the nation's
second-largest planned city experienced an increase of
1.5 degrees Celsius in its annual temperature average.
Many of the plants and animals that lived there died out
or retreated; in their place, I put down my roots. Even my
long-standing symbiotic friends raced neck-and-neck to
accompany me. The people of the planned city neither
welcomed nor shunned me and my friends. News about us
came up a few times in their papers and news broadcasts

but the reality was they were too busy to pay us any mind. Silently we learned to adapt to the soot and noise.

Once he had observed me so diligently and now he had no time to pay me any attention. That's how busy he was. He wasn't busy because of his research. He was busy ghostwriting papers for others or teaching writing classes intended for the general public. Apart from that, he was busy treating professors to expensive alcohol at bars that overlooked the river, wheedling them to recommend him for a job. Or busy clicking into one university homepage or another. Or busy watching sports and drinking beer in his studio apartment. The anthropologist did not like his life in the new city, which was divided up evenly like a chocolate bar. Since there was no chance the universities in the capital city would hire him, he'd decided to trust in his distant relatives' connections and settle here, but in reality there wasn't much they could do to help except buy him a drink. So, he was often drinking.

The anthropologist did not blame Rabi for the way his life had turned out. All she'd done was tell him the stories she knew; he was the one who had misunderstood and misused them. Sure, the project had fallen apart after she'd taken the money and run, but she hadn't broken her promise. Yes, Rabi had taught him how to neutralise the purple bean's poison in exchange for money and, yes, later it had been shown not to have any medicinal properties, but she hadn't lied. Never once had she claimed the liquid would have any pharmacological effect.

The anthropologist had been the one to push on ahead against the odds.

He had believed that with a plausible excuse he would be able to count the money he'd spent on Rabi as a research expense. But the botanist, thinking Rabi had fled because of the anthropologist's rash behaviour, reported him for misusing research funds. After begging forgiveness from his principal investigator and the board of the research foundation, the anthropologist had managed to avoid criminal charges, but he'd had to recoup the amount from his own pockets. His wife had divorced him in the middle of all that too. But that was for the better, he supposed. Their relationship had never been that great in the first place.

So everything had been his mistake. He knew that. Whenever he talked about those days over alcohol he couldn't help but spew, *Fucking bitch, fucking bitch*, but he didn't truly harbour any malice toward Rabi. Plenty of people said bitter things they didn't mean while drunk.

Except he flashed back to his memories of Rabi. A young woman like a strong young sapling. Skin like the bark of a rubber tree. Dark, solemn eyes. The song-like intonation of the old language that flowed effortlessly from her lips. When he heard her speak, he felt like he was speaking to Rabi's mother, her mother's mother, and her mother's mother's mother. He felt the memories that no one remembered slowly surging through him. Like quicksand. Like a tidal wave. Like time.

If only he could hold fast to those memories. The anthropologist felt a deep regret. If he hadn't been so hasty with Rabi, if he hadn't let her slip from his grasp, he would've discovered so many more truths. He couldn't shake his regret at the thought of it.

When the anthropologist met Rabi again, it was by pure coincidence.

The hagwon had cancelled classes for the day because the building needed repairs done, so the anthropologist was wandering about downtown to kill time. He held a bottle of beer in one hand and had been tipsy since early evening. Glancing at shop signs before him, the tablet computer displays in the shop windows and the headlines flashing above the newsstands, he kept snickering. He was in a good mood. Eventually he came across a building with a neat, modern exterior that looked similar to the hagwon where he worked. Embedded in one of its white-painted walls were these letters made of deep-blue aluminium: *Mind Academy*. He was already primed to snicker, but this time he let out a snort of laughter. On the bulletin board below the name, a large poster had the current month's curriculum printed on it with these types of course: Philosophy for the Modern Person, Farewell to Alcohol, Crying Practice, Aromatherapy: From Foundation to Application (*students get 50% off all aroma oils*), Talismans and Feng Shui (*students get 50% off selected dowsing rods and crystals*), Knowing Yourself Through Tarot (*tarot deck included for all students*), Meditation with Nature in the City . . .

The instructors' profiles were just as ridiculous. Each one had studied at some dojo in Japan, or some shrine in Tibet, or done interdisciplinary studies at some university in Ireland. Some had studied under a famous guru, some claimed to be descendants of the Romani, and there was even someone who described themselves as an independent researcher of ancient civilisations. The instructor for the meditation course had a particularly notable background:

> *The last true shaman of the D tribe, an indigenous people from the South. Offers long-standing wisdom on commun- ing with nature to awaken one's mind and heart.*

The anthropologist snorted once more and the corners of his mouth turned down. He stared for a long while at those sentences and at the instructor's photo beside them.

To coincide with the hours people left work, the medi- tation class took place from 8 to 9.30 p.m. The anthropolo- gist seated himself on a nearby bench and waited. Rabi might've already been in the building because 8 p.m. came and went and he hadn't caught sight of her entering. So he waited longer. The darkness deepened and the air grew cooler and more humid. Streetlights blinked on here and there along the streets, illuminating night-time in the sub- tropical city. The anthropologist emptied another bottle of beer. At 9.37 p.m., people began streaming out of the building. They greeted each other amicably, laughing at each other's jokes; some of them broke off in groups and headed toward nearby bars while others headed off alone in their own direction. All of them looked happy.

At last Rabi descended the stairs of the building. She was wearing a blue minidress and sandals. The magenta beads dangling from her belt twinkled, drawing the eye with each step. Her gait nimble and breezy, Rabi unwrapped what looked like a piece of candy or a caramel with one hand and mumbled something to herself. No. She had AirPods in her ears and was talking with someone.

'Yeah, I just finished class and am on my way out. All right, see you soon.'

Rabi's pronunciation was flawless, save for when her mouth puckered because of the candy or caramel. She wore light make-up on her face, and it looked like she had had some work done.

The anthropologist stayed seated on the bench. He didn't know what he should do. What he should say. Still clutching the empty beer bottle, he got to his feet without much of a plan.

Rabi was walking toward her car, which was parked in the wide lot in front of the building. The lights in the building were all turned off, likely because she had been the last to leave. There was only one silver four-wheel drive within the boundaries of the parking zone. Rabi was bending her head as she fished around for her keys when suddenly, as though she had noticed his presence, she swung her gaze toward the anthropologist. She squinted, searching the anthropologist's face.

'Who . . . ?'

At the clear look of betrayal in the anthropologist's eyes, she hurriedly added, 'Were you a student of mine? I'm sorry, I'm not very good with faces . . .'

Rabi could not continue speaking. The anthropologist had smashed his beer bottle into her head.

The anthropologist straddled Rabi's collapsed body and struck her head and face several times. *Fucking bitch, you fucking bitch, you scamming bitch*, he spat. There was no one around to hear him.

The anthropologist's hand finally stilled several minutes

after Rabi had stopped breathing. Suddenly he was sober. His face turned pale with fear. He picked up as many glass fragments as he could and stuffed them into his pockets. Then, swaying on his feet, he fled the scene.

Rabi had no relatives. The academy management didn't even know exactly where the D tribe was located, much less how to get in touch with Rabi's village. They only expressed their reluctance at being questioned by the police; and, because they wanted to avoid unnecessary media attention, they didn't mention anything about a 'shaman' or her 'extinct language'. The investigation dragged on at snail's pace and was eventually declared a cold case. This was no surprise, given that most murders of indigenous people were handled this way. A few of Rabi's friends and students collected some money and held a simple funeral for her. Her body was buried at a public cemetery. On her tombstone were written the words: *Here Rests Our Teacher*.

One year later, from Rabi's grave grew new plants that had never before existed in human history. From her breasts, her rear, her genitals, her feet, her hands, a different sprout germinated, a stem stretched upward, and a new leaf grew. Flowers of all new shapes and scents bloomed and the plants bore fruits that no one had ever before tasted. But no one visited the grave, so no one knew of this except for us.

# Welcome to the Alps
# Grand Park

Ask anyone to name a place with clean air and the first location most people will come up with is the Alps. Canada, Finland and Iceland are popular answers too, but no image is more potent than that of the snow-capped peaks of the Alps – with a crisp breeze blowing through ridges packed with freezing blue glaciers and Heidi romping through meadows among the heady fragrance of fir trees. Swarmed year-round as they were with fine dust particles in the air, Koreans imagined they would find in the Alps their homeland's beautiful autumn landscape, lost long ago. In reality, thousands of Alpine glaciers had melted away due to summer heatwaves over the past several years.

When the government first installed air purification towers in fifty-eight locations across the country and revealed they would be developed into 'clean air zones', the competition to name these zones grew as stiff as the bids for construction work. If each zone's facilities were going to be more or less the same, a captivating name that could attract visitors and revitalise the local economy would at least be a simple point of differentiation. Naturally 'the Alps' flooded all the 'Name Your

Neighbourhood Clean Air Zone' contests – everyone was eager for the zone they lived in to become the Korean Alps. Eventually, the one to hoist the flag of victory was the Alps Grand Park of N City, located at the edge of Gyeonggi-do.

Unlike what its name suggests, the Alps Grand Park is not very big. It comprises a community park, which was once beside an old apartment complex and the site of a defunct thermal power plant. The original park's landscaping was left mostly untouched, but a new walking path was built to connect the park to the power plant. In order to meet the clean air zone requirements, the land was also planted densely with trees, with a wide-open plaza centred around the air purification tower. The Alps Grand Park is built like any other clean air zone, with a parking structure equipped with charging stations for LPG and electric cars, a fitness centre, swimming pool, tennis court, playground, performance centre, marketplace, and not to mention numerous food stands, restaurants and cafes – everything that the folks who'd held off going outside due to the fine dust were now eager to enjoy. The scenery is not quite as beautiful as the real Alps. There are no mountains or rivers or lakes, and certainly no glaciers. There are no places to camp like there are at Blue World in Gangwon, or at Pristine Lake Park which makes up part of Jirisan National Park. But that is not to say the Alps Grand Park doesn't have its own unique selling point – namely, the Miru Art Centre, an art museum on the site of the old thermal power plant. Preserving the power plant's original structure, this hip space is a place for young up-and-coming artists to exhibit their work. The wide outdoor courtyard, which is perfect for admiring installation art from every angle, is also a popular date venue for young couples. At one point, it was trendy to share photos on Instagram of the defunct power plant's now-dead smoke-stack in contrast with the bright-white air purification tower and its blue bird logo in the background.

The air purification tower, which is a good ten armspans wide, is striking to view at a distance but also certainly worth seeing up close. This is because of the rollable display that wraps around the tower like a belt, sitting at eye level for the average adult. With a touch of the screen you can peruse real-time air quality metrics and weather reports; maps and information about the surrounding facilities; park visitor numbers; and general information about the government's environmental policies and pro-tections. You are also able to use eco-mileage to charge the battery in your mobile devices and buy tickets to the art museum. The large display screen halfway up the tower shows the current time as well as the volume of dust parti-cles purified by the tower in real time. Somewhere around the seventh or eighth floor of the tower, another display shows the news and advertisements. There are captions running along the bottom of the screen, but if you connect to the tower via Bluetooth you will be able to hear the sound as well.

Even today, all around the vicinity of the Alps Grand Park air purification tower, people stand still, walk by, or sit upon benches, with or without earphones, watching the display. The following captions float across the screen:

> **... Reduction measures in place following days of elevated fine dust levels ...**
> **... Mean density to exceed 1,300 mg ...**
> **... All advised to conduct business within clean air zones or buildings equipped with air purification systems ...**

'No wonder it's so crowded,' mutters an elderly woman, looking up at the screen.

The woman is wearing a purple windbreaker and trainers. Judging from the small backpack slung across her back, the handkerchief tied around her wrist and the dark sun visor pulled over her forehead, she is, by anyone's estimation, a woman out to get some exercise. A non-stop stream of young couples dressed in the latest fashions and families on outings with their children pass her by. She squints up at the blue sky over the brim of her visor. Under the scatter of cumulus clouds, a fat pigeon flutters into the autumn air.

'Well, how am I supposed to know what the weather's like out *there* if I'm living here?' the woman mutters to herself once more, sweeping an eye over the bustling crowd in a displeased fashion.

The woman, Kyungsook, makes her way to the only empty bench in the vicinity, pulls out her water bottle from the outer pocket of her backpack, and takes a mouthful. The sweat soaking her hair trickles steadily down her temples.

Kyungsook has a habit of saying she 'doesn't know what the weather's like out there'. What she means is that she has only ever lived in the Alps Grand Park apartments so she has no way of even knowing how hazy the air is in other places. She may sound like she's frustrated by this, but in fact it's something she is proud of. It emphasises just how pleasant and comfortable her life is. When Kyungsook's son and his wife call, she tells them, 'Goodness but I have no idea what the weather's like out there', and at Sunday church, when she discusses the results of her government-provided lung cancer screening with her friends, she says almost dismissively, 'Oh, you know, it's because I hardly know what the weather's like out there', as though that were the foundation of her good health.

There is a reason for Kyungsook's distinct pride in her neighbourhood: for almost thirty years she lived in the old low-rise apartments that were once here. When her husband first bought the place, she didn't know a single thing about real estate. She didn't even know that it wasn't necessary to buy a place near the thermal power plant just because her husband worked there. As a native of N City who had worked for many years in the power plant control room, her husband took great pride in his roots and his job; Kyungsook, as his wife, simply thought it natural to honour that sense of pride. When she told their son proudly that his appa made the blood flow through the veins of the nation, her husband's face looked more attractive to her than any film actor she'd ever seen. Kyungsook imagined her sons growing up like their father and scrubbed and scrubbed the dress shirts and school uniform shirt collars stained black with particulates until they were white. This was a time before anyone could predict that the Covid-19 pandemic of 2020 would shake the nation's blood vessels to their core.

They had only just paid off their loans when the worst possible economic crisis hit. The government shut down all thermal power plants and shifted their energy policy to focus on nuclear energy. Her newly unemployed husband sank into a depression like that of a soldier back home after a war. While his compatriots with plenty of energy, plenty of time to spare or nothing at all staged protests, Kyungsook's husband acquainted himself with lethargy and the liquor bottle; and Kyungsook, now needing to provide for her sons' college tuition and living expenses, found herself battling at the front lines of her household. Her now-unreliable husband had a foul temper but he did not whine, although sometimes he lashed out when bitterness got the best of him. In any case, regardless of what anyone said, her husband had lived his life with such diligence and yet the world had just abandoned him. Kyungsook steeled her heart with the compassion she had for her husband and the love she had for her sons. She drew much strength from her trust in God, that He would one day deliver her from these tribulations.

When it was revealed that this area was to be developed into a clean air zone, Kyungsook was convinced that God had answered her prayers at last.

With a smile on her face, Kyungsook gets up from the bench. She settles the backpack once more on her shoulders and leaves the tower plaza, now following the walking path. Her pace is quick and her arms stick out in a disciplined manner. A brisk jaunt while maintaining proper form eases her headache considerably; it will likely help with the distinctive twinge she's feeling in her knees lately too. The fact that she is this healthy – despite inhaling such bad air in her youth and despite how tough her life once was – is all thanks to God's grace. Kyungsook continues along the walking path winding around the park, gazing fondly at the elegantly maintained grass and trees. Looking at the royal azaleas lining the path in full bloom and the deciduous trees iridescent with unshed raindrops, she is filled with a satisfaction almost like she personally cultivated this land.

There is nothing more that Kyungsook could desire. In her shiny new remodelled apartment, Kyungsook cranks up the heat in the winter and the air conditioning in the summer such that there is no way to know the actual weather on the outside. She cooks and eats whatever she wants to eat and watches whatever she wants to watch on the television. This is how she lives her life. Her two sons married women who were not entirely up to her standards, but decent enough. Not only will she never again have to worry about putting bread on the table, but she has a house that she can leave behind to her sons, and the value of that house will only continue to rise. The only thing she has to complain about is the vacant spot left behind by her husband, who passed away far too soon. She wonders what her husband would think if he could see this world with her – this world in which air quality is an important measure of life quality; in which the government, aiming to redistribute the population in order to limit the spread of infectious diseases, erected air purification towers in underdeveloped parts of the country, thus causing housing costs in those areas to skyrocket.

'No, no. He'd only have something nasty to say if he were still alive.'

Shaking her head, Kyungsook rounds a corner. She cannot imagine her conservative husband getting used to life in this new day and age.

Eventually, a slightly elevated wide-open space spreads out before Kyungsook. It is installed with ellipticals, stationary bikes, bench presses and a variety of other exercise equipment. Most of the equipment is already being used by other people. Kyungsook, who was planning to use the 'rolling waist' machine like always, stops walking and knits her brow. A woman she has never seen before is standing on the machine and twisting her body so violently that her torso practically folds in half. That's not a machine she should be using if she doesn't properly know how. What if it breaks at this rate? Kyungsook worries, her nerves on edge.

Kyungsook finds the outsiders who flock to the Alps Grand Park to be an eyesore. They're careless about throwing out their trash. They ruin public property. They walk on grass that they're not supposed to walk on. And they're always so loud. If actual residents of the commercial district can't enjoy the benefits they're entitled to because of outsiders, what is even the point? Kyungsook wonders whether she should suggest to the Residents' Centre that the park exercise equipment only be available to residents.

Who knows, some people might have the impudence to come here every day like they're commuting to work, just so they save on gym memberships! Kyungsook once lodged a complaint after being alarmed at the sight of a dozen or so homeless people who had made camp in a secluded spot behind the art museum's ticketing office. Seeing them act so brazenly like it was their territory, drinking coffee – and not the instant kind from a vending machine, but a franchise take-out coffee, no less – and playing hwatu, Kyungsook felt a deep contempt. How hilarious that even in those circumstances they wanted to drink their Americanos and breathe in the clean air and hadn't the slightest bit of shame at sleeping on the pavement. Some people work hard and save like hell to get what they want and others dare to just laze around and sponge off them.

Kyungsook leaves the exercise equipment and goes back toward the walking path. She corrects her posture and begins walking again, now in the direction of her apartment.

She sees a man and his dog approaching from the other side of the path. Thinking him to be another outsider about to let his dog poop in the flower bed and leave without bothering to clean it up, she glares at him.

... **Professor: Significant correlation between air pollution and neurological disorders** ...

... **Photochemical reaction of fine dust found to release toxic tertiary byproduct** ...

... **Recent air pollution disease epidemiology and national response strategy** ...

Jinwoong, who was checking his email on his phone while his dog sniffed around, raises his head, suddenly feeling the prickly heat of a glare on the back of his neck. A few metres away, a woman around his mother's age is staring at him. He meets her eyes, vaguely wondering what her problem is, and then turns back to his dog, Albami. Albami's nose is shoved into a bush, sniffing intently. Another dog seems to have urinated there.

The woman draws closer at a rapid pace and the stiff expression on her face begins to soften noticeably. She greets Jinwoong in a dramatic show of delight. 'Aigoo, I was wondering who that was! Aren't you the doctor from the hospital just over there?'

Jinwoong puts his phone back into his pocket and grabs Albami's leash. 'Yes, hello. I'm so sorry, I don't believe I recognise . . . ?'

'Oh, I came by the hospital with a friend last month to get a brain scan. Because of my awful headaches. So you live here? You don't look like the kind of person who'd have a dog.'

'I see . . .'

Jinwoong attempts to respond with the appropriate amount of respect. He is, in fact, exhausted and in a very bad mood right now. He has no desire to chit-chat with patients outside of the hospital, when he's not even on the clock. Thankfully, the woman seems to notice Jinwoong's sour expression and quickly adds, 'You must be busy. I don't want to take up your time. Please do be on your way', and takes off along the walking path, swinging her limbs vigorously.

Jinwoong watches the woman's retreating back for a moment. From her tacky clothing to her coarse skin and boisterous way of speaking, she did not give off the air of a wealthy elderly woman. Jinwoong thinks she seems more like an outsider who's travelled here from afar to exercise than a resident of this place. He sees so many outpatients each day at the university hospital's neurosurgery department that it is impossible for him to remember the faces of each and every woman like her. And the number of patients keeps increasing as the days go by. He might even die of overwork, at this rate.

Jinwoong follows Albami, who has trotted some distance ahead. Albami is a four-year-old Boston terrier. Jinwoong named him that because the maroon splotch on the white of his pudgy puppy face reminded him of a chestnut. Nowadays he's so busy that his wife is the one to take care of Albami most of the time; so, naturally, Albami too likes his wife more than him. At the very least Jinwoong takes his dog out on walks on his days off – but the little punk doesn't appear particularly pleased to have Dad as his travelling companion.

'Consider yourself lucky, bud,' Jinwoong snaps. 'You think all dogs have it as good as you?'

Albami turns a deaf ear and only tugs on the leash in Jinwoong's hand, marching forward briskly like a general returning home from a successful military campaign. Whenever Jinwoong takes Albami on a walk, he realises just how fortunate he is to live in this neighbourhood. It is clean, safe and well paved, so he can take his dog out without worry whenever he feels like it. If he lived in the 'shaded zone' of the air purification tower, he wouldn't even be able to dream of such extravagance. Of course, residents of the shade resign themselves to living there no matter how bad the air is, so they probably walk their dogs in that air too without much thought (or perhaps they don't take their dogs out at all). But Jinwoong knows better than most just how noxious the fine dust can be to children, the elderly, and even dogs.

When the general public think about the fine dust problem, most associate it with respiratory disease. They also vaguely understand that fine dust can travel through blood vessels to cause organ inflammation and cell damage, thus triggering cancer, diabetes, stroke – really any kind of disease. What many do not know is that it can also cause epilepsy, Lou Gehrig's disease or even Alzheimer's.

A variety of opinions surround the recent rapid increase in idiopathic neurological disorders among the lower class, but there is no doubt in Jinwoong's mind that fine dust is at fault. It's obvious that the toxic particles comprising fine dust impair the central nervous system in a specific way. The symptoms – cyanosis; severe convulsions; nausea; excretion of sweat, tears and mucus; and, in severe cases, loss of consciousness or transient loss of vision due to seizure – are similar to the body's response to organophosphate exposure. Similar, in other words, to the effects of nerve agents used during World War II. The government is trying its hardest to divulge information without alarming the public, but the day any media outlet says something about this being similar to the chemical weapon used in Kim Jong-nam's assassination, the impact will be massive.

The fact that this phenomenon dates back to approximately four years ago is very ominous to Jinwoong. It might mean that, four years ago, industrial complexes in Korea and China started to emit a new pollutant. Or that the toxic agents that had accumulated in people's systems over the years and failed to break down had passed some critical threshold and were now abruptly causing the aforementioned symptoms. If not that, then perhaps it's due to, as the Society of Air Pollution Disease's email newsletter put it, 'toxic tertiary byproducts' of a photochemical reaction. If that's the case, it will be nearly impossible to find a solution. All these man-made chemicals permeating the air, interacting with one another to create a Frankensteinian abomination – how is one supposed to stop that? It's beyond humanity's control. At least, not without the government installing five hundred more air purification towers to clean the air of the entire nation . . .

But this country does not have such astronomical amounts of cash. That much is obvious when you see how the government fights to raise taxes even just marginally because its budget barely covers the maintenance of the existing towers' filters.

'Seriously, you better know how lucky you are,' Jinwoong stresses once more to Albami as he pulls a waste bag from his pocket.

Albami glances up at Jinwoong, bored. *Hurry up and pick up my poop*, his gaze seems to say. Jinwoong sighs and scoops the warm lump of faeces into his bag.

Must be nice being a dog. They say that dogs have no conscience, nor any sense of inferiority or guilt. Unlike for humans, a dog's happiness isn't relative. They don't compare themselves to other dogs' situations and feel unhappy. All they ever want is to eat good food, run around and play to their hearts' content, and spend time with their owners.

Jinwoong thought he would start to feel happy when he was selected by lottery to own a place in the Alps Grand Park Ecoville. He had studied until his nose bled to become a doctor and endured his time as an intern and a resident, resisting the urge to rage-quit multiple times a day. He thought he was finally being rewarded for all those years of sacrifice. But, despite moving his marital home to a new place and becoming a respectable medical specialist, Jinwoong is not happy. All of his friends have set up their own clinics in Seoul or in their hometowns with their parents' aid and are raking in hundreds of millions of won from the cushy comfort of their offices, where they behave like fortune-tellers who only ever tell people what they want to hear. How long does *he* need to keep at it like a salaryman, unable to sleep, plagued by the need to work overtime?

Honestly, he sometimes resents his parents. He knows how hard they worked to support him but if only they had been just a little bit better off – it's hard for him to shake the frustration he feels. Moreover, whenever he thinks of them, Jinwoong becomes caught in a tangle of emotions, from resentment to guilt to fondness, all jumbled together. While his parents do live within the air purification tower's radius of influence, they are not residents of the 'tower district' at the centre of the clean air zone like their son.

The air quality where they live is rated 'Satisfactory', but it certainly is not as clean as that of the Alps Grand Park.

How is he taking a dog for a walk in a clean air zone, and not even able to get his own parents a decent house in the tower district?

Sunk in these gloomy thoughts, Jinwoong eventually finds himself at the front lawn of the Miru Art Centre. He comes to a halt and gathers himself as Albami yanks his leash taut. There is a retriever in the distance panting excitedly and trying his hardest to race toward Albami. 'Slowly, slowly!' the retriever's owner cries. She tries hard to take control of the leash but looks like she is being dragged forward instead. Jinwoong smiles to indicate it is all right to approach, and allows Albami to greet the retriever. The two dogs circle each other, sniff one another, wag their tails, and then, having hit it off, begin to romp and play.

They were right back in the day with that old proverb. *A dog's life is the best life*, Jinwoong thinks as he glances around at the installation art on the front lawn of the art centre. As always, there are young couples on leisurely strolls, taking photos with their phones.

Good times.

Jinwoong's lips curl into a bitter smile.


'How could you be so narrow-minded? Of course they need to be compensated by the government. It's not like people living in the shade live there because they want to. And they're not sick because they want to be sick either!'

'I'm just saying, you have to be realistic. Is there actual proof that those people got sick because they live in the

ROADKILL

shade? No one knows for sure. It could be because of their family medical history or lifestyle . . .'

In front of an exhibit that is a mountain of PET bottles – hard to tell whether it's trash or art – a young man and woman bicker with one another. Both of them are in their early twenties. The man is wearing a college varsity jacket and jeans and the woman has on classy make-up and a dress.

Still arm in arm with the man, the woman replies brusquely, 'They'd know that if they did the research. That's part of the government's responsibilities. They shouldn't have been so discriminatory when they built the air purification towers in the first place. The prejudice is right in front of your eyes! The residents of shaded zones are having their fundamental right to health violated.'

'There's no such thing as the *right to health* in the Korean constitution. Seems like you should know that as a law student.'

'Ugh, you . . . !'

The woman, Harin, raises her voice in frustration but finds herself choking on her words. The man, Sungkyu, remains calm. Sungkyu looks at his girlfriend pityingly and shakes his head. 'Let's move on. You're getting too worked up. Jesus, we shouldn't be fighting about politics, of all things, on our date.'

Sungkyu starts to move away first. Behind his back, Harin's lips flex as if she wants to say something else, but eventually she resigns herself to following along beside him, a sulky expression plain on her face.

Sungkyu finds this side of his girlfriend more than a

little irritating. Harin joined some sort of environmental activism group last semester and started spewing all kinds of bullshit. It's like she got brainwashed by all those vegetarians and feminists and activists and went crazy. She says she won't eat ramyun anymore because it contains beef and milk, and that she won't get her driver's licence because she vows to never use a car, and that she has no time to go on dates because she's attending anti-nuclear-power rallies. They were on a date for the first time in a long while at an art museum in the Alps Grand Park, but they got into a fight when she went on a fiery rant about airborne microplastics – right in front of an exhibit that warned of the environmental harm caused by plastics.

Sungkyu cannot comprehend what grievances a girl from a well-off family, with a pretty face and a killer body, would have that would make her act this way. Harin has more than enough money to not come to these public facilities with their corny names. This is a girl who auto-tops-up her Seoul 'Secret Garden' membership card with 1,000,000 won each month and doesn't think twice about going there for a walk or to take advantage of exclusive services – like being able to adjust the artificial sunlight, clouds, fog and rain – on days she's feeling a bit stressed. In truth, Sungkyu is glad that thanks to her he doesn't have to worry too much about paying for dates. If she could just stay still and keep her mouth shut, everything would be perfect.

Granted, the news these days is in complete uproar about 'gangshi disease'. Named after the stiff, hopping corpse of Chinese folklore, the disease – developed frequently by children of lower-income families – causes the face to turn blue and the body to move unnaturally, like a convulsing gangshi. There's a guy in Sungkyu's department with it. He started convulsing during a lecture one time and caused a huge commotion. The kid had never once let it slip that he was from the shade and he always went around in expensive clothes, so it was even more of a shock. It's true that kids from poorer families do tend to show off more than others, in any case. With their circumstances now improved, they're quick to flaunt their lifestyle at every opportunity, but their impoverished past always finds a way to make itself known.

With this in mind, it's clear why government compensation for gangshi disease patients living in the shade is completely illogical and unrealistic. It's not just people living in the shade who are developing gangshi disease. It's not just poor people who are developing gangshi disease either. Even someone who's lived their whole life in a clean air zone could get it if they're unlucky. They might have been exposed to toxins somewhere and not even known it. Plus, it's not like that's the only disease that's caused by the fine dust. Suppose the government did give gangshi disease patients money because they took to the streets in a furor. Then all the people in the shade with lung cancer, high blood pressure, asthma, corneal inflammation, depression and even schizophrenia might start demanding compensation too. Even if most of them would've developed those diseases regardless of the fine dust.

Sungkyu pulls Harin along to where all the restaurants and cafes are located. Harin is in a mood and says nothing. Sungkyu will not bother trying to make her feel better.

She's probably even more peeved because she's hungry. Once they have some good food, she's bound to get tired of fighting and let go of her anger herself.

'What shall we eat?' Sungkyu asks when they arrive at an elegant plaza adorned with European-style sculptures and fountains. In the centre of the plaza there is an Italian bistro, a fast-food place, a Thai restaurant, a Japanese restaurant and a sandwich shop all in a line.

Their signage and decor may vary but every restaurant has outdoor seating. They are alike in that respect because people visiting a clean air zone for the first time in a while will, of course, want to have their meals outdoors while enjoying the sunlight and fresh breeze. Harin and Sungkyu are no different. Harin looks around carefully and then points at an empty table in front of a wood-fired pizza restaurant. 'I heard the pizza over there is good. They have a vegan pizza too.'

Harin hurries past Sungkyu and sits down quickly before the spot can be taken by someone else. Harin's expression looking at the tablet menu on the table has already softened considerably. But at the thought of Harin ordering a fake pizza with vegan cheese and only toppings like mushrooms and aubergines, Sungkyu, on the other hand, is pissed off again. Back in the day when they went out to eat, they always ordered something they could share, and since Harin never finished her food as a matter of course, Sungkyu always ate one and a half portions. But now, nothing Harin eats tastes any good, so not only does he *not* want to share her food but whatever food she gets is several thousand won more expensive than normal food.

Harin, of course, has no sense of money, so she's totally fine with paying for her own meals, but Sungkyu is the one who has to go with something cheaper on the menu. He's the one who has to pick out cheap gifts. He's the one who has to try his damnedest to find discounted hotel rooms, all the while pretending he's unbothered by it. He's sick of it. If only she could take a hint like other girls. Oh, I just feel like eating some gukbap today. Let's just go to a motel nearby – how nice it would be if she'd say something like that.

'I'm going to get this and the grapefruit-ade.'

Sure enough, Harin is pointing to an image on the menu of a pizza covered in grass and mushrooms. Of course, Sungkyu thinks, and draws the tablet toward him. But he lets his eyes linger on Harin's cleavage, peeking above the neckline of her dress, reflected on the glass of the tabletop – and allows himself to be comforted.

'Shrinking the greenbelt to build rental apartments? How does that make any sense? I mean, this is a so-called "clean air zone" – wouldn't you want to plant more trees, not cut them down because you want more people moving in? I'm telling you, this is something all the apartment residents need to come together to protest. I have no idea what the president is thinking. Why don't they just make more clean air zones?'

A highly strung woman in her late thirties who is sitting outdoors at a cafe, across from the wood-fired pizza restaurant, is on a tirade. Opposite her, another woman who looks a few years younger is staring vacantly at the pizza restaurant, only half-listening. Specifically, she is looking at the young couple seated outdoors at the pizza restaurant, at the letters on the back of the young man's jacket.

*Jisan University, Department of Business Administration.*

The young woman eating pizza with him is probably also a student at the same university.

Whenever the woman, Yoojung, sees students from prestigious universities, her heart automatically fills with longing. What would it feel like to spend one's youth at a good school like that, to study there, even to date? Yoojung is well past the age to attend university – she's already a mother to a daughter in first grade – but she still feels a profound regret. Perhaps she, too, could have graduated university. If she hadn't given birth to Hyuna . . .

Hyuna tugs on Yoojung's sleeve. 'Umma, Umma, I'm bored.'

Yoojung turns to her in surprise, startled that Hyuna seems to have heard her thoughts. Hyuna, in turn, is looking up at her mother, her lips in a pout, appearing to be incredibly bored. On the table before her is Yoojung's phone and an empty ice cream dish next to it. Soomin, who is sitting across from her, is fully absorbed in a game she's playing on her mother's phone.

'Oh my, your daughter doesn't play games, does she?' Soomin's mother exclaims with an expression that is half amazement and half appreciation, while Soomin simply keeps her eyes glued to the phone. Hyuna is smart enough to realise that Soomin Umma has praised her and hides shyly behind Yoojung's back.

There's definitely something funny about Hyuna. Unlike

other children, she likes books far more than smartphones. From a parent's perspective, it's a good thing, but in some ways it's also a bother. You have to read aloud to her, choose books for her and answer all of her questions. With other children, all you have to do is hand them a smartphone and they keep themselves entertained. You don't even know they're there. Yoojung picks up her phone, opens up a children's book broadcast channel on YouTube, and offers it to Hyuna. But Hyuna, who seems annoyed or upset about something, looks like she is about to cry. 'I said I already saw all of this,' she whines in a tiny voice. Yoojung suppresses her temper and steadily goes through her other subscribed channels. At last, Hyuna finds a video she likes and her face brightens as her gaze fixes on the screen.

'How nice for you that Hyuna's so clever. She talks back so clearly, with such confidence too.'

The slight barb in the other woman's words sets Yoojung's nerves on edge. 'Oh, not at all. I think she just likes books. She's not interested in anything else, really . . . My husband and I worry about her.'

'I'm sure. Teaching social skills is important too. Isn't it tough, all that we need to handle as mothers?' Soomin Umma says with an indecipherable smile. Yoojung gets the sense she is secretly being sarcastic, but doesn't know what exactly she's being sarcastic about. Maybe she's saying in a roundabout way that Yoojung can't fit in with the other mothers of this neighbourhood? Or maybe she's criticising Yoojung for being unable to properly raise Hyuna?

Yoojung suspects that all the ladies around her, including Soomin's mother, know that not only is she just a high-school graduate, but that she's also from a shaded zone. She doesn't have proof, but she can feel their gazes, their whispers about her. Tentatively, she turns the conversation back to their original topic. 'That's so true . . . I'd also worry about Hyuna mixing with those, um, kids from the rentals. You never know who your child will be playing with at school . . .'

'Exactly!' Once again worked up, Soomin Umma takes big gulps of iced Americano and adds, 'As it is, those people give me such a headache, what with drying chilli peppers on a mat in the middle of the park, pushing through hedges because they don't want to walk around the flower garden . . . Imagine what children from those kinds of households learn from watching their parents. It's obvious, isn't it? Now, my darling Soomin has always gotten along so well with everyone since kindergarten, and there was one time . . .'

Soomin Umma launches into a story about a problem Soomin faced in kindergarten with the kids from the rentals. She's told this story a couple of times already but Yoojung keeps her expression neutral. The fact of the matter is that the majority of families living in rental units are from shaded zones and this conversation is nothing but a way to badmouth people from the shade. The house Yoojung lives in is her husband's property so she never thought to bend the knee to people like Soomin Umma, and she wants to associate with them even less. That's the truth. She privately regrets bringing up this topic but it is too late.

'Come to think of it, I don't know if you've heard of this

but there's something called gangshi disease going around these days.'

At Soomin Umma's words, Hyuna abruptly looks up and then back down. This is when Yoojung realises that Hyuna has been pretending to be occupied by the smartphone, and all the while listening to their conversation. What could she be thinking in that tiny head of hers? Yoojung wraps an arm instinctively around Hyuna's shoulders.

'Gangshi disease? What about it?'

'There's a rumour that it's contagious.'

'What?'

Soomin Umma lowers her voice and says in a whisper, 'It's spreading in the shade but the government is apparently trying to keep it under wraps. They're focusing on human patients mostly at the moment so not a lot of people know this, but I heard a huge number of animals are dying off too. Apparently, if you go somewhere like O City, you can see corpses of street cats and mice all over the place! Just thinking about it makes my skin crawl.'

Hyuna lowers her hand holding the phone and glances at Soomin Umma. It turns out that Soomin, too, has abandoned her phone on the table and is looking up at her mother, her chin tucked into her hand.

'Really? I thought they said it's because of the fine dust . . . Couldn't the animals be dying because of pollution as well?' Yoojung says carefully.

Soomin Umma lets out a fake cough, suddenly conscious of the curiosity and fear in the children's gazes. 'Who knows? In any case, there's no harm in being careful. If we happen to catch the disease while hanging around too close to sick people, we're the ones who'll suffer. You be careful too, Soomin.'

At her mother's words, Soomin glances sidelong at Hyuna and Yoojung with an odd expression. Taking in the peculiar look of guilt clouding Soomin's face, Yoojung is certain once more. The children know everything.

Without a word, Yoojung hugs Hyuna around the shoulders again. Almost as if she could protect Hyuna this way.

'Ugh, whatever. Let's just go. We just need to admit that we lost it and all they'll do is scold us a little.'

'Still. Let's keep looking around a bit more. I mean, it *is* school property.'

In the sparsely developed woods along the back of the cafe, two girls wearing their school gym uniforms are walking around carefully while bickering. One girl is taller than the average adult and has a strong build, while the other girl is chubby – she follows behind her friend reluctantly, dragging her swarthy calves step by step. The tall girl, Eunjin, stoops to survey the ground, pushing aside the quince and the stubby lilac trees. No matter where she looks, the fluorescent yellow-green tennis ball remains out of sight.

Chaeryung sighs. 'So weird. I wonder where it went off to. It's not like we're in the mountains or in a big forest with a ton of trees that it'd be this difficult to find a ball . . . Hey, you don't think a dog ran off with it? I saw a man walk by with his dog just now . . .'

Eunjin listens in silence to Chaeryung blathering on and her footsteps come to a halt. 'It's probably over there. Don't worry about it too much. Stuff like this can happen when you're practising.'

At Eunjin's calm tone, Chaeryung's mouth snaps shut. Eunjin most certainly said that out of consideration for her, but it only makes Chaeryung feel worse. They came all the way here on a weekend to practise tennis because of Chaeryung's inferior skill. And, of course, they lost the ball because Chaeryung's bizarre serve sent it flying over the hedges of the tennis court. She can't forget the expression on Eunjin's face the moment the ball sailed through the air and vanished: a look of disbelief mixed with resignation, as if she hadn't expected any better.

Would she actually improve with practice? Chaeryung wonders. The more she hits the ball, the more the strength drains from her arm until the racket feels as heavy as a stool. She feels bad that she might be dragging Eunjin down. But Chaeryung can't say that to her. And Eunjin doesn't let the inconvenience show on her face either.

The two girls look through the grass for some time. Even though all they've done is walk into the flower garden, everything is quiet, as if they are a step removed from the outside world. The footsteps of people in the plaza, the voices of people at the cafe, all seem to come from far away. The tennis court they left empty seems to be occupied by another pair now, for they can hear the cheery *thwack* of a ball hitting a racket at regular intervals. Chaeryung listens to their effortless sounds and tries to guess their skill level. Then she wonders if she'll ever be as good as them.

Not by a long shot, of course. Chaeryung and Eunjin's school has only just started a tennis club and they're a motley, ragtag bunch, from the coach to the club members. Chaeryung included. Eunjin might be different since she's played tennis since elementary school, but it's pointless for her to do her best at some school in the shade – not like that would get her into university anyway. Chaeryung simply went along with Eunjin and joined the club without much thought. But the moment she saw the glitter of ambition in Eunjin's eyes, she felt bad about not taking it more seriously.

'I hope we get a tennis court at school soon. Don't you?' Eunjin says as she uses the end of her racket to rummage through the weeds while in a squatting position.

Eventually the two girls arrive at an empty patch of land in a remote area. Perhaps there were once plans to plant something or build a facility here, but the square patch of soil has been neglected for so long that it is thickly overgrown with weeds. In comparison to the tidy, well-manicured gardens near it, it appears even more squalid.

Grateful the silence has been broken, Chaeryung immediately adds, 'Definitely. It's so annoying packing up our gear and coming all the way to a clean air zone to practise. Makes me feel self-conscious. Plus they won't even allow us in the park if it gets too crowded . . . It's super annoying.'

As she speaks, Chaeryung grows more and more animated. Eunjin gets up and dusts off her clothing, saying, 'Oh yeah, did you hear they're not going to allow people with gangshi disease into places like this anymore?'

Chaeryung gapes at her. 'What? Why?'

'I think they think it's contagious or something. I dunno, could be fake news. I was looking at the school community page and that's what everyone was posting about. Stuff about precautionary measures.'

'Oh my god, that's crazy. Like, don't you only get that disease if you're poor as fuck?'

Chaeryung snickers as she thinks about those blotchy blue gangshi kids. The two or three gangshis from each class came together naturally as a group and always hang out with each other. This is because all of them are overly sensitive, depressing or too pathetic to get along with the normal kids in class – although it's uncertain if they've become that way because of gangshi disease or whether only kids like them develop gangshi disease. Sometimes Chaeryung wonders how on earth the gangshis are able to stand each other's personalities when they all hang out.

'Speaking of which, I'm glad there aren't any gangshis in the tennis club. We shouldn't let them join in the future either,' Chaeryung says. She digs at random through the weeds with her racket, almost unconsciously. The edge of her racket catches a PET bottle cap, an empty snack packet, a corn dog skewer, a dirty wipe and other such things, and sends them flying. An orange Fanta cap goes rolling across the ground until it hits Eunjin's calf. Eunjin grins and kicks the cap back toward Chaeryung.

'That's rich. We let kids like you who can't even hit a ball join.'

Chaeryung bends down to hit the cap with her racket but misses by a hair's breadth and the cap rolls through her legs and off into the distance. Twisting around to follow its trajectory, she discovers something strange.

'Huh, what's that?'

She walks over to what looks like a blue stuffed toy lying next to the cap. She hears the rustle of Eunjin approaching behind her. Chaeryung crouches to get a better look at the blue object and then lets out a little scream.

'Look at this!'

'What is it?' Eunjin looks over Chaeryung's shoulder.

It is a dead pigeon. The pigeon's feathers are a deep-blue colour, like that of a bluebird from a fairy tale. It appears to have died a while ago, for the mice and insects have already eaten parts of it, leaving only a hollow carcass behind – but on top of its blotched, rotting surface and bones, the blue feathers are as vibrant as poster paint.

For a moment, the two girls stare down at the carcass without saying a word. They cannot look away, even as they are filled with nausea. Eunjin moves her foot slightly and several ants passing by disappear under the sole of her shoe. Several others march rapidly by, out of the flower garden surrounding the two girls and toward the plaza.

The plaza that was once the sports grounds of a neighbourhood park by an old apartment complex is paved with concrete blocks of dark and light grey. On top of them, a great many people go about their day, drinking in the clean air as they enjoy an afternoon of leisure. In front of the food stands, restaurants and cafes, there is a wide area of outdoor seating with tables at least two metres apart from each other, where people eat and drink and make conversation. The trees – thoughtfully planted to foster harmony between flora and fauna as well as naturally suppress the proliferation of pests and weeds – show off their verdant green colour and their fresh scent. There are no mountains or rivers or lakes, and certainly no glaciers. But when the smokestack of the Miru Art Centre – built on the site of the old power plant – and the blue bird logo on the bright white air purification tower behind it are against the blue of the sky, they make for quite the impressive landmark. Visible from anywhere in the park if one only glances upward, the air purification tower's large display shows the current time and the volume of dust particles, as well as news from a public broadcast station. No matter how much the mean density of fine dust particles rises, the air quality of this area will always read 'Excellent'. Even on the day the last glacier in the distant Alps melts into nothingness, the weather in this place will be as fair as can be.

This place is the pride of N City: The Alps Grand Park.

# The Door Scope

## 1. The Dressing Room

'Once you've lived in a new apartment like this one, you'll wonder how you ever managed in the other,' my husband says to me. His words brim with certainty, never mind that this is his first time living in a new apartment building too.

'Look at this. You can control the electricity in each room with this tablet.

'When a package gets delivered in the lockers outside, it'll send you an alert. This is great.

'You can even link the home system to your phone. Take a look at this.'

My husband looks like a boy as he alternates between touching the screen embedded in the wall and his smartphone, a serious expression on his face. Despite being seventeen years older, whenever my husband is excited about something he looks far younger than me. I pause in the middle of putting away our clothes and turn my eyes toward the phone in his hand. There is a blue house icon on the screen.

'Say you forgot to turn off the gas before leaving the house. All you need to do is go to the app and do this and this. You can easily check on it and turn it off. Convenient, right? I imagine it'll be quite useful for a scatterbrain like you.'

My husband smiles impishly at me and I smile back at him. He has a handsome face. How optimistic he is for our future. Everything will get easier for us in this house, he says. Our married life will change for the better. We'll be so much happier than before. He is trying his hardest to instil in me that same confidence. I do not want to betray my husband's efforts.

'Yes, it's wonderful. Our safety won't be a cause for concern at all,' I say. Of course, it is my husband who will be using his smartphone to remotely turn the gas on or off. I don't own a smartphone. I don't have much reason to spend long hours alone outside our home either. In his glee, my husband appears to have overlooked this fact.

Suffering from severe depression and anxiety means I spend most of my day in a state of extreme lethargy. Not only do I lack the energy to go out, but I find it terrifying to be among people I don't know. It feels like everyone is mocking me. Every other person is a normal, respectable member of society, each one bringing their own unique value, while I alone seem to be a pathetic, useless piece of human trash. We have been married for six years already and I still do not have the nerve to bear him a child. I do not work, nor do I socialise with friends. I spend all day at home watching Netflix, reading books, spending money on home shopping channels and being a burden to my husband. I am always in such a daze that, even inside the house, I often forget where I put things and fail to adjust the gas range and thermostat. How uneasy my husband must feel to leave a person like me alone all day while he is at work! How upset he would be to see me drifting through the house like a phantom, with a grim expression on my face.

When he was looking for our new house, my husband took a number of factors into careful consideration for my sake. It needed to be someplace quiet, far from the main thoroughfare, so as not to overstimulate me. Someplace close to a park, a nice spot where I could go for a walk or a jog. Someplace highly secure so I would be safe even when I was by myself. What's more, it was to be a place worth investing in for our future. That place turned out to be in this newly built apartment block in this new city.

Because the area was just starting to undergo development, it was rather empty. There were no places like coffee shops or supermarkets or florists to be found; there were more real-estate offices than convenience stores, more cafeterias for construction workers than casual eateries. With a wintry wind blowing through its neatly arrayed, barren saplings, the 'park' was more like a vacant lot. There were no sounds of children playing or dogs barking. One after the other, the ground-floor glass windows of shops yet to open lined the streets of the shopping district, standing empty like aquariums without water, waiting for people. At the mouth of the road leading to the apartment complex, employees of wall-plastering and home-cleaning services and the like stood passing out flyers with phrases like *Congratulations on your move!* and *Wishing you every success!* written on them. New land, new life. A benediction to erase one's shabby life of old, as though none of it had ever existed, and to live a dazzling new life. Just like the new city had erased the old city, with traces of all the people who had ever lived there removed, as if they had never existed at all. Just as it had built all of these gleaming new apartments, new studios, new buildings.

No, that's too cynical and exaggerated of a metaphor. I need to stop thinking like this. Hasn't my husband criticised me for using too many metaphors? He's been saying that since before we were married, when I was still his student and he my professor.

Let's focus on the present.

That's what the psychiatrist advised me to do too: not to get caught up in thinking about the past, but to focus on the present. At the moment, we are putting the house in order. While my husband inspects the smart home system, I am unpacking the bundles of clothing that the movers haphazardly shoved into the wardrobe and arranging them by type and season. This is the dressing room. It is the first time I have ever lived in a house with a dressing room. The dressing room is furnished with a large full-length mirror, along with built-in shelves and clothes racks that span three walls, and a steam closet. My husband is very particular about his attire. He always says that just because you're a writer doesn't mean you should be going around in a crumpled undershirt, giving off the stench of cigarettes and soju. When you are neatly attired, students regard you with authority and trust you when you stand before them at the lectern; you will not be looked down upon by your fellow professors or publishing professionals or government officials. I could not help but agree with my husband's words. After all, when we were dating, his sense of style was one of the reasons I was attracted to him. In the dresser drawers and on clothes hooks I arrange my husband's shirts, neckties, gloves, socks and handkerchiefs by how often he uses them. I like the smooth feel of his silk ties, the scent of leather emanating from his gloves.

I have far fewer clothes than my husband. This is no surprise, given that I have no social life of my own. Still, my husband is not careless of my attire. Every once in a while he will take me to the department store on the weekend and buy me elegant outfits, typically in colours like ivory, beige, black or grey, with shoes to match. For my birthday or our wedding anniversary he will even buy me things like luxury-brand watches. I am grateful that my husband cares so much about my attire even when I have no reason to go out except to accompany him as his wife. But then I feel ashamed, wondering if I am so ugly that he finds it mortifying to be seen with me unless he dresses me up like that. I keep feeling like the luxury brands my husband buys for me do not suit me. My husband tells me they suit me perfectly fine but I do not think that others think this. I bet they think things like, 'Someone like *that* is wearing a Van Cleef & Arpels wristwatch? Talk about casting pearls before swine.' I bet they think things like, 'No matter how hard she tries to act refined, she can't hide what she's truly like.' 'What's worse, that ivory jacket makes her big breasts look even bigger.' 'She looks so dim-witted.' I bet they think things like that.

'Darling, come over here. Take a look at this,' my husband calls for me from the living room. I hang up a jacket on a clothes hanger and step outside.

My husband is standing in front of the large tablet embedded in the marble of the living room wall. On the screen is a small, rather dark image.

'This right here is the outside of our house. You can see whatever's happening right outside the front door in real time while staying inside.'

I stand beside him and look at the monitor. Separated by a narrow hallway, I can see the front door of the apartment directly opposite us. The camera does not capture the elevator that's on the left or the staircase landing and window that are on the right. Only the door of the house in front of us stands apart, visible to the camera.

'If there's someone suspicious creeping about or you hear something strange, you just have to turn this on like this to check. And if you press the button next to it, you can record what's happening too. Pretty amazing, huh?'

I do not think it is particularly amazing. I wonder if I'll have a use for technology like this. After all, the front door has a door scope. If anyone comes, I'd find it more comfortable to go up to the front door, look through the scope and open the door myself.

'That's incredible. Technology has come so far.'

'Indeed.'

'Still, after checking who's outside from here, I'll have to go up to the front door to open it. It would be nice to have something like a housekeeping robot to open the door and bring guests into the living room.'

I am making a joke, but my husband does not appear to find the joke very amusing. His eyes narrow somewhat and, with an unconvincing smile, he presses buttons here and there on the tablet and starts showing off some other function.

I bite my tongue a little. This is how unsociable I am. I don't even know how to make a casual joke that others will enjoy.

My husband does everything for my safety. He wishes for me to not be hurt by this world or by other people. He feels responsible for my unhappiness or sadness. But in my life, *I* am the single biggest threat to my own welfare. There is no security camera, no strong and sturdy front door, no lock between me and myself. I cannot chase myself away from me. All day, every day, I intrude upon myself. That is what frightens me.

## 2. The Study

My husband is a tenured professor in the creative writing department of a national university located in the capital. He was able to be appointed to this position despite his young age because of his achievements as a literary critic, but also because of the strength of his personal connections and family. His father is a poet and scholar of Korean literature and his mother is a pianist, while his paternal grandfather was vice minister at the Ministry of Culture, Sports and Tourism (at the time known as the Ministry of Culture). Theirs is a highly elite family. I cannot even fathom what it would be like to grow up in a family like that. Maybe their home was filled with books, their afternoons echoing with classical music. Perhaps, during meals, they would discuss the latest aesthetic theories from Europe, a glass of wine in hand. Although my husband's family did not bring up such complex topics when they met me, I did wonder if they were choosing their words because I was there and they were being considerate of me. They are cultured, in other words.

My husband's study is quite different from the old hardwood study that was my father-in-law's, which I caught sight of at their home. At my husband's request for a modern feel, the interior decorators matched the bookshelves and desk with black-and-white steel and marble. There is a grey herringbone-patterned rug spread out on the floor and, on top of it, a large desk bearing a computer. Scattered on his desk are the academic journals my husband is currently reading, as well as books gifted to him by his juniors and by publishers.

On nights like this one when I can't sleep – nights like these are frequent – I often spend time in the study. My husband is not pleased with my presence in his study but I can't help it. Watching television at night makes my head hurt. Plus I should not disturb my husband's sleep, so I can't do anything too noisy. They say that if you can't sleep it's best to relax your body and lie still in bed, but if I were to do that and wait for sleep to come, I would be overwhelmed with bad thoughts. So, I wait for when my husband is in deep sleep and slip out of bed.

In the chill air, clutching my cardigan close, I pick up a novel by a contemporary Brazilian writer that I was reading on and off yesterday, and walk toward the easy chair. But another book lying on the tea table in front of the easy chair catches my eye. Under the desk light, the pink-and-black cover sticks out like a stage prop that doesn't match the rest of the study. The sentimental title too: *Good Night, My Morning.* I flip open the book. Inside the cover, in even handwriting, are the words *To my professor, with respect,* followed by a woman's name.

This is something that happens from time to time. A student who has taken my husband's class publishes their debut work and then gifts him a copy of their book in gratitude. And, of course, while not explicitly mentioned in the dedication, that includes a request to read the book and write a favourable review.

I look over the novel's table of contents and the blurbs on the back cover. I skim through the pages of the book with my fingertips. The pages are clean. My husband has either not read this yet or, if he has, he's treated it very carefully.

I wonder whether this student has a crush on my husband. I'm not sure what it's like these days, but when I was in school many female students apart from me liked him. He was at the peak of popularity among the general female readership too, in fact. From the blistering criticisms that made up his newspaper column to the romantic, confessional tone of his essays, as a writer my husband had a fluent command of language that appealed to the masses. His face might not have been considered attractive, but his tall, immaculate frame and his elegant attire made him stand out everywhere.

Our relationship was a scandal that rocked the literary world. There was our age difference and the fact that we were teacher and student, but also the fact that, from my very roots, I was completely different from him. I grew up in a broken family: I had no father, my older brother had run away, and my mother ran a pub. Since I had no one to emulate, I had no taste. I read whatever I could get my hands on, without any standards; my clothes I bought online or by the roadside, according to whatever was in fashion. I consumed alcohol and cigarettes like there was no tomorrow. When I think back now to my campus life, none of those days stand out in my memory. They all blur together. I wasted time drinking every single day with my peers and upperclassmen, making stupid jokes, gossiping about others, reproaching the literary circle, talking about K-pop idols and movies, discussing other people's relationships. Eventually I myself became the subject of gossip and slander and rumour. When a classmate and I got wasted and went to noraebang together, betting on who would sing more songs, we ended up having sex. The very next day, rumours that we'd had sex spread throughout our department. Once that happened, the upperclassman I was dating dropped my manuscript from the anthology he was editing and said he never wanted to see me again. I took a leave of absence and started working part-time at the school library. A close friend of the upperclassman I had been dating came to see me at the library every day, asking me to go on a date with him. I dated him. Not long after, I caught my current boyfriend telling my ex-boyfriend over KakaoTalk that I was 'a bitch with great tits who pays for all my shit'. I heard that a sex tape of me was being passed around. I didn't want to know the details. I took another leave of absence.

I might never have gone back to school if it hadn't been for my now husband. If it hadn't been for the text he sent me then, the one that read: *I miss your writing. See you in class* . . .

Abruptly, I come to my senses.

I got caught up thinking about the past again. Let's focus on the present. I lower the book back onto the table and listen carefully to my surroundings. There is an odd noise coming from somewhere. An *oooong* sound, like something vibrating. It sounds like it's coming from somewhere lower, somewhere beneath my feet.

I am standing still and holding my breath, so the sound gets louder and louder.

I remember that this is a new apartment building, one that I have moved into. I realise what that sound is. It is the sound of the elevator ascending. The study is adjacent to the elevator shaft, and where the easy chair and table are situated is especially close. Because the apartment building doesn't have many residents yet, it is natural that the sound of the elevator moving in the dead of night would be so loud. It is like the sound of a giant crane moving.

I press my ear against the wall and listen. I can hear the sound of the cable connected to the elevator grinding against the pulley, clear as a bell. I think I can even guess roughly which floor the elevator is on. My husband said this house was built with high-quality materials so the sound insulation is great. Given that I can hear what's happening outside so distinctly, that does not seem to be the case. But who is taking the elevator at this hour? I heard only two or three other households had moved into this building aside from us. This is the nineteenth floor, the very top floor.

The elevator stops at the top floor.

When I hear the cheerful *ding* sound, I leave the study. I cannot hold back my curiosity. With hurried steps I creep up to the front door and press my eye to the door scope. Through its curving lens, I see the door of the house opposite us.

Then, in front of the door, I see the back of a young woman appear.

The woman has her long hair tied back and she is wearing a purple silk dress. In the dim hallway, that vivid purple dress looks so intensely bright that it does not seem real. The woman does not enter a passcode for the door lock, nor does she insert a key into the keyhole. She simply stands there.

Perhaps two seconds later, the door to the house opposite us opens.

The woman steps inside. The door closes.

Everything becomes quiet.

## 3. The Dining Room

'Darling?'

After a moment of hesitation, I sit at the dining table. My husband is reading the news on his smartphone and spooning siraegi soup into his mouth.

'Hmm?'

'You know the house opposite us? Has someone already moved in there?'

'No. It's still empty,' he says, indifferently scooping up a bit of rice and placing it in his mouth.

'But someone went in there last night.'

My husband's chopsticks still.

'Who? When?'

'When you were asleep. I was having trouble sleeping so I got up and went to the bathroom . . . and heard the elevator outside. I got curious so I looked through the door scope and saw some woman going into that house.'

'Some woman?'

'I don't know. A young woman. I only saw her from the back. She was . . . wearing a dress. A silk dress.'

My husband furrows his brow. 'A silk dress? In this weather?'

I shrug. 'That's what I thought. It's strange, isn't it? She must've been cold without a coat . . . Also, that dress, it felt like I'd seen it somewhere. It seemed really familiar. Maybe you'd know? It was this deep-purple colour, with a scooped back . . . I think it was a halter neck . . .'

'Don't be silly. You must have been mistaken.' My husband cuts me off flatly, but his tone is gentle. It is the same voice he uses in class when a student says something wrong during a presentation. For a moment I think he is referring to my observation that the woman's dress was a halter neck. Then I realise he is disclaiming her existence itself, the young woman I saw with my own two eyes. 'That house is empty. And it's the middle of winter,' my husband declares, as if stating an obvious scientific fact.

I say nothing. Somehow, I am angry at my husband. But I cannot explain my emotions logically.

His expression softens slightly. 'Are you sure you weren't dreaming?'

'It didn't seem like it.'

'You didn't take your medicine yesterday, did you?'

I start to protest, and then stop. I search my memory. Did I miss a dose last night? I must have, since I can't remember.

'The pills in the bottle were untouched. That is not good, darling. You have to make sure to take your pills so you can sleep well.'

'. . . I haven't hallucinated anything so far.'

'I know, I know. I'm not saying you hallucinated, I'm saying that you may have made a mistake while you were half-asleep. You might've had a night terror. A new house can be disorienting, can't it?'

My husband begins to move his chopsticks again. This time, he puts the jangjorim in his mouth. After that, he eats the bean sprouts. Since my husband keeps to his Korean-style breakfast every day, the refrigerator must always be stocked with basic banchan dishes. On the other hand, I have no appetite at all in the mornings. I begin wondering whether there is a banchan shop around here.

'Or maybe it was a ghost,' my husband teases.

I laugh out loud.


## 4. The Bedroom


My husband said the novel I'd written contained a rape fantasy. That was my debut novel. It was controversial too. In a bad way. I had written a novel that dealt with the sexual experiences of a young woman, no more, no less.

Then, of course, people tried to read my novel as autobiographical, but that sort of misunderstanding didn't worry me. I knew I needed to tell that story even if it caused a misunderstanding, and so I did.

I no longer remember why I felt that need.

In any case, my husband – who was my professor and lover at the time – said my writing was good and told me to submit the novel to a literary prize for new writers so that I would be able to make my official debut into Korea's literary circle. I submitted my novel, and was chosen as the winner.

Up to that point, there were no malicious rumours surrounding my winning the award. My husband was not on the judges' panel for that publication and our relationship was secret. It was only after I'd made my literary debut and safely graduated from school that he made his relationship with me public and began prepping for the wedding. That was sensible of him. People only recalled after the fact that my husband's close friend had been on the judges' panel and they knew there was a high chance that my husband had asked him to consider my work favourably. That level of suspicion alone wasn't enough to dent the legitimacy of my winning. People didn't care much about legitimacy, in fact. They were only interested in knowing how I had seduced my husband in order to make my literary debut – or how my husband had seduced a naive young woman with promises of making her debut. Stories came pouring out about my appearance and body, my promiscuous college days, my list of ex-boyfriends; about the secret looks my husband and I had exchanged in class; about dating while I was still in school.

Aspiring writers who failed to make their official debut whined that they were losing out because of people like me who had a pretty face and knew how to play the game; not only that, they made cursed predictions that, even if someone like me did debut, I'd run out of capital soon enough.

My husband simply ignored these rumours. He made no official comments on my book either. People expected my husband to say something in that distinctive, elegant style of his that divulged his true feelings, but he was not so easily swayed. He always acted like a gentleman.

He only spoke about my novel in bed.

'You slut.'

My husband shoves me onto the bed. I get up and pretend to run away.

He grabs me by the hair and throws me across the bed again.

'Stay fucking still. I can snap your neck in two.'

He sounds so vicious that, if someone were to overhear, they'd think he was serious. I shouldn't do as he says, though. If I listen to him, it won't be rape. In order to act like I'm being raped, I need to pretend to resist. I need to struggle, I need to say no, I need to beg him to stop. If possible, I need to cry. If I happen to shed tears, my husband feels a deep remorse. He apologises to me so tenderly. Then a languor washes over me, like I'm sinking endlessly in tepid bathwater, dark as pitch. To me, that is like orgasm.

I crawl onto the rug sprawled under our bed. My husband drives his foot into my back. I gasp for breath. He applies more force with his foot. I writhe. My elbow throbs in pain. I must have hit it somewhere when getting down from the bed. My husband climbs on top and inserts his penis into me. I let out a cry that's almost a scream.

It's confusing sometimes. There have been times I've felt like I'm really being raped. What we're doing is consensual, of course, so it's not rape. I know it's not. I know it without a doubt, and yet. There have been times I've felt, unshakeably, that my husband won't stop no matter what I do, that I'm not *pretending* to fail at resisting him, but have always been failing, and that, at this rate, he may actually kill me. And if he were to try to kill me, no one would help me, and my death would have no effect on anyone whatsoever.

I steel my mind. I must not think depressing thoughts. If this keeps up, I'll start crying. Or maybe I should cry? Should I sob and scream? It seems like that would fit the role too. But would that agitate my husband? Wouldn't that ruin things?

'Keep quiet,' my husband says.

I bite my lip and let out a groan.

I decide to turn my attention elsewhere. Not to the present, but to another time. I think of the past.

That's right. My husband said the novel I'd written contained a rape fantasy. The narrator *appears* to be shining a light on male violence by showing us scenes of the female main character being raped by various men. But, in fact, the narrator herself is *enjoying* telling the story that way. Citing Lacan's theory of something or other, he dissected my novel's narrative technique and spoke of literary works from Europe which were twisted sex fantasies. He told me that my novel was just as shocking and engaging as them.

I listened to his words with interest. It was fascinating that he had discovered something that I myself had never once been aware of, never once intended. I preened to learn that my professor, whom I respected, had such regard for my novel.

As he said this, my professor fondled my breasts. I found his touch intoxicating. That was in his office, and I was alone with him, surrounded by his books.

'I consider literary criticism fundamentally a form of love. I fall in love with a work, and this is an act of confession. But loving you with a mere confession is not enough. I want to give you an even greater kind of love.'

As he said this, my professor pushed me down on top of his desk. He blocked my mouth with his hand. And then . . .

Suddenly I open my eyes.

I must have fallen asleep while we were having sex. Or did I pass out? I can't remember. My husband is fast asleep in our bed. I rouse my body, which has fallen flat on top of the rug, chilled to the bone. It is so cold. Is the heater working?

I put on my bathrobe and go to the kitchen. Bleak moonlight spills into the living room through the bare glass windows that are still without curtains. With all their lights off, the other apartment buildings look like giant gravestones enveloped in darkness. I fill a cup with warm water from our water purifier and drink a little, warming myself up. My hand is shaking.

Now that I think of it, did I take my medicine this evening? My medicine, I need to take my medicine. Then I'll be able to sleep again. I walk over to the kitchen shelf where the medicine bottle is.

Right then, I hear the sound.

The sound of the elevator ascending. The vibration that sounds like *oooong*. Even though this isn't the study, it still sounds loud and clear, as though it is right by my ear.

I creep up to the front door.

The elevator makes a *ding* sound. After two or three *click-clack* sounds of footsteps, a woman walks into the field of the door scope. A woman with long hair tied in a ponytail, wearing a purple silk dress.

I stare carefully at her back.

I see a strap and ribbon traversing the nape of her neck. So it is a halter dress. The ribbon around her neck hangs down low on her back. Something shiny and metal is dangling from the ribbon. Yes, it definitely feels familiar. It's a dress I've seen around often. But where? If only I could see her face . . .

As soon as the thought crosses my mind, the door to the house opposite opens and the woman disappears inside.

Before I know it, my body stops shaking.

## 5. The Bathroom

I didn't tell my husband about what happened last night. But I did think about it all day. Even while I washed the dishes, even while I sliced up the kimchi and packed it away in airtight containers, even while I put our freshly washed comforter into the dryer.

On and off, I thought about it even as I wiped stains of my husband's come and piss from the toilet seat. And now, while I stand in a pouring stream of water washing my hair, the thought seizes my mind more strongly than ever.

Where have I seen that dress? Did I see it on a mannequin in a shop window or a character wearing it in a TV show? Maybe a lost memory, buried deep in my subconscious, of something I once took a fleeting glance at, is now suddenly giving me déjà vu? But it felt too familiar to be that. It didn't seem like a piece of clothing I'd merely chanced upon and then disregarded. It felt like someone really close to me, maybe even I myself, had once worn a dress like that. It felt like the dress and I shared some personal history.

I rinse off the shampoo and squeeze conditioner into my hand. The elbow that I hit on the bed frame last night keeps throbbing. I turn on the cold water and point the nozzle of the shower head toward it, trying to cool the heat.

But, wait, let's go over it again. That's impossible. The dress was something like an evening gown that a celebrity might wear to a cocktail party. I've never been anywhere that would warrant an outfit like that. I've never been close to anyone who'd wear a dress like that either. And it's nowhere near the style of outfit my husband would buy for me, with its overly flashy colour, its shimmering, glossy fabric, and the design that left the back fully exposed. When my husband sometimes watches those year-end award ceremonies and sees actresses wearing dresses like that, tottering down the red carpet in stilettos, he expresses his scorn. 'An actress is the modern-day equivalent of an upper-class gisaeng. Just look at that gaudy outfit,' he'll say, and eye their breasts.

With conditioner in my hair, I squeeze shower gel onto

the bath sponge and make it foam. I look down at my body. I pinch my belly with one hand. I have a habit of checking my body for extra flab every time I shower. I heard that, if you stand straight and press the crook of your thumb and index finger into your side, palm up, and are able to grip your flesh, you have too much flab. I'm not sure where I heard that, though. In any case, my husband always stresses that the worse my mental health is, the better care I should take with my body and my routine; that if I sleep too much and binge-eat and gain weight and don't wash or clean up because of my depression, I'll become even more unhappy. I think he's right. What I need are rules in my life. At the very least, I try to maintain my shape enough to fit properly into the clothes my husband buys for me.

When I think about clothes, I think again of the purple silk dress.

I search through my memories. Could there have been a time when I was a student that I was drunk or momentarily crazy enough to buy something like that? Back then, I spent money so indiscriminately that it's very possible I blew my wages from my part-time job on such a ridiculous item. If that's the case, that dress would have been the first to be included in the bundle of old clothes I threw out before getting married. I threw out the hodgepodge of household items I'd accumulated while living with roommates, and the cheap clothes, the worn underwear, the useless books and old diaries and stacks of letters. I wanted to erase the me of the past. My husband knew of that me, but thankfully he pretended otherwise; he thought me a vulnerable, somewhat simple-minded girl who, as a result, had made a few mistakes. I wanted to live up to his generous assessment. I might not be able to delete the sex tape that was going around, but I could sort out what was around me. I might not be able to fix all the past mistakes I'd made, but I could fit my life cleanly into my husband's space.

As I rinse off the soap suds, I hear a knock on the bathroom door. I turn off the water.

'Yes, darling?'

I hear my husband's voice over the *drip-drip* sound of water falling from my hair. 'Finish up quickly and come out. I need to talk to you about something.'

I wonder what urgent matter could have come up. Hastily, I rinse out the conditioner and, after soaking up most of the moisture with a towel, put on my bathrobe.

I open the bathroom door.

My husband is standing in front of the door with a stiff look on his face.

'Follow me.'

I tie the sash of my bathrobe, twist up my hair in a towel and put on my slippers in one fluid motion and follow my husband. His footsteps are quick. Water droplets drip onto the floor of the hallway, shadowing my footsteps. My husband enters the study and sits in the easy chair.

'Have you been going into my study again?'

I stare blankly at my husband, still standing. He picks up a book with a pink-and-black cover from the tea table. *Good Night, My Morning.* He flips open the book and shows me the pages that are crumpled and torn. There are tattered pages between crisp ones, as if someone has deliberately tried to ruin the book.

'You did this, didn't you?'

I do not answer.

'Who else would it be, if not you? In this house.'

I do not answer.

'I told you not to touch anything in my study unless you're cleaning up. Especially my books.'

'I'm sorry.'

'I told you, books aren't good for your mental health. Think of all the books these days that are full of strange content. The characters all say the craziest things. They inflict self-harm. They kill themselves . . . If you read things like that, you'll start coming up with bad ideas. Do you know how much I worry about you?'

'I know.'

'Don't tell me you want to start writing again?'

I do not answer. My husband sighs.

'You know you're not ready to face the literary world yet. How are you supposed to appear before them the way your mental health is? You said you find it difficult even to talk to grocery store employees. To think of putting your writing in front of those cruel rumour-mongers . . . and what about all the comments people make on the internet? It's too horrible to even imagine.'

'I know.' As I watch a fat water droplet fall in the direction of my foot, I add, 'If I wrote a few things now, I could gather them up and publish them later, couldn't I?'

'Now? Write what, exactly? You don't even know what's trending in books these days. And you have nothing worth writing about around you either,' my husband says, flapping his hand lightly. Then he grabs my hand and, meeting my eyes, he says my name in a low, tender voice. 'Let's do our best to get through this. We moved here, didn't we? I was promoted and got a raise too. Everything is going to be all right. Things will only get better and better from here.'

I flex slightly the finger that's grasped in my husband's hand. I can feel the deep wrinkles carved into my husband's large, warm palm. In my head, I can picture the lines making up those wrinkles.

'It's still winter and the building just started taking tenants so it feels desolate now, but soon, when there's more people and the weather warms up, it'll feel more lively. Do you know how pretty the park is here? The city really made an effort. I hear the cherry blossoms will be phenomenal in the spring.'

'Okay.'

I dip my head so I won't have to look at my husband's expression and pretend to retie the sash of my bathrobe.

Everything my husband is saying makes sense, but I don't know why I feel so hopeless. My husband worries for me and cares for me, so why do I hate him so much? I didn't even say I was going to write, I didn't even dare to make that resolution – how could he say all that to me? I can't write. I have no talent. If it hadn't been for my husband, I wouldn't have been able to debut at all. I have no intention of diving into such a hopeless endeavour and consuming myself. None. Then why?

My husband gets up from his seat, walks over to his desk and brings me something. It is a cup of water and a pill bottle. My husband, who worries that I, with my memory problems, will forget to take my medicine on time prepares a morning pill bottle and an evening pill bottle for me and fills it up with the medicine I need to take every day. If the bottle is empty, I've taken my medicine; if there's medicine inside, then I haven't. Before my eyes, my husband opens the bottle labelled *Evening Medicine*. Inside, there are five pills, both large and small.

'Here you go, time for your medicine. Take your pills, dry your hair and get some rest.'

While my husband watches, I put the pills in my mouth, take a drink of water and send them down my oesophagus.

I don't know why I dislike taking my medicine so much.

## 6. The Living Room

My symptoms grow worse. I do not have the energy to do anything except lie on the sofa. Even running the vacuum is beyond my power, so I often lie sprawled on the ground, and taking out the trash feels as deadly as walking through lava. Lying on the sofa, I turn on Netflix and shut my eyes, not watching or listening to any of the content. I hear the sounds of some apartment being moved into, sounds of machinery from the studio apartment construction site, the bellows of the workers to one another. Right when I think it has become quieter, the sun sets and it is night-time.

My husband says I'll get better. But, at this rate, what if I just get worse and worse? I worry that I am, in fact, hallucinating. My husband has not brought up the woman in the purple dress again, as though it's something I said in passing and he's forgotten it. But I can't forget even for a moment. Eyes closed or open, the back of that woman flickers in front of me.

No matter how I think about it, it's probably true that this is all a hallucination. According to my husband, that house is empty. Not only is it improbable that someone would wear just a thin dress in the cold of winter, they wouldn't keep wearing the same outfit every day either. And no matter how quiet the nights are, it doesn't make sense that the elevator sounds would be heard so loudly. Nothing I see or hear at night is reality.

I think through what I'll say when I visit the doctor next week. I don't even have the energy to get up and grab a pen and paper to write it down. I'm hallucinating things, Doctor. That's never happened to me before. My forgetfulness is getting worse and worse too. My emotions are all over the place. The smallest things make me miserable. I'm scared, Doctor. I'm taking my medicine properly. My husband manages it for me to make sure I don't forget. The day I forgot to take my evening pills, I hallucinated so . . .

Speaking of which, it occurs to me that I have not yet taken my evening pills.

I sit up on the sofa. It is already past midnight. My husband said he wouldn't be coming home tonight. He was going to some conference in the countryside. With my husband gone, my sense of time feels even more disjointed. My stomach growls. Recently I haven't been eating properly either.

I step onto the marble floor with my bare feet and walk to the kitchen. I take out a loaf of bread from the freezer, let it thaw a bit and then use the sharp-edged bread knife to cut two thick slices. I put the slices of bread in the toaster. I take out strawberry jam and peanut butter and a small carton of fresh milk from the refrigerator. After smearing peanut butter and jam onto the golden-yellow bread, I stuff my mouth with the sandwich, still standing at the kitchen counter. I put the milk carton to my lips and take a drink. It's been a while since I've had milk from a single-serve container. I remember how we used to get milk like this distributed to us in elementary school. Suddenly I feel a little better.

I take a tub of chocolate ice cream back to the living room sofa. I shovel ice cream into my mouth with a large rice spoon and switch the television on to a public broadcast. There is a travel show in full swing.

The show is about a group of celebrities travelling to overseas tourist destinations with a limited budget and enjoying their travel as frugally as possible. I watch intently as they count coins outside a famous tiramisu shop in Venice. I must have fallen asleep without realising it because, suddenly, a strange noise wakes me up. As soon as I wake, the first thing I think of is that I skipped my evening medicine. I should have taken my medicine before sleeping. I stand up from the sofa. And then I hear the noise again. The sound of the elevator ascending.

I stay rooted to the spot, unable to do anything. The sound continues. I'm hearing things. No matter how much I repeat that to myself, the sound slowly gets louder and clearer, as if mocking me. This isn't real. But try as I might to turn my mind from it, the sound does not seem to disappear.

Trembling all over, I walk to the front door. I press my eye against the door scope.

The elevator halts with a *ding*, the door opens, and I hear footsteps coming out. But this time, it's not just one person. Mixed in with the *click-clack* sound of shoes, there's the sound of a different tread. One that's a bit heavier, a bit lower . . .

Before long, the woman in the purple dress comes into sight.

And a man comes to stand next to her.

He is a tall man wearing a suit. His face isn't visible but his body is leaning at an angle toward her, so I see his necktie.

I know that necktie well. A deep-blue silk necktie with a diamond pattern. I know what fragrance emanates from that necktie as well. Because I am the one who sprayed it.

The man and the woman step through the door of the house opposite and I stay standing still until the door shuts. I don't know how many minutes, how many hours, might have passed.

I put on my slippers, open the door just wide enough to slide out, and approach the house opposite. I put my eye to their door scope. But I can see nothing but darkness.


## 7. The Balcony

Could my husband be deceiving me?

Could he be deceiving me and cheating on me? With the woman in the house opposite ours? Or maybe using that empty house as an easy hideaway? Has he been seeing another woman right opposite the house he lives in with me? A woman who wears a purple silk dress like an upper-class gisaeng. A woman who publishes books with ambiguous pink-and-black covers. A woman who is younger, fresher, more talented and more beautiful than me.

What kind of sex fantasy might my husband have read in that woman's novel?

Yes, I know. That there is a good chance this is all just paranoia. The scene I witnessed yesterday through the door scope might just be a hallucination. Maybe, after being deceived by my own fantasies, my mind is now developing even bigger delusions.

If I assume that my husband is having an affair, however, everything fits. Including her only ever wearing the purple dress – it makes perfect sense if my husband asked her to wear it whenever they have sex. Also, the fact that my husband always makes me take my medicine to put me to sleep. Also how angry he got at me because I rifled a bit through that book *Good Night, My Morning*. And how he comforted me afterward. And . . .

Staring into space and thinking intently, I lean my forehead against the railing of the balcony. The thin clumps of snow on the railing melt quickly and dampen my forehead. The fevered heat in my head feels like it is cooling down. Over the railing, a snowy expanse stretches before me. Blanketed in snow, this wasteland of a new city, with nothing but buildings and young trees, does not look very different from the old parts of town. Two or three children run about in the snow, leaving behind footprints. Their parents follow, keeping a careful watch. When we first moved in, there wasn't a single family with children among the other tenants. A new elementary school is said to be opening in the new year, so it seems like this place, too, will soon be bustling with children. Normal couples love each other, fight with each other, make up with each other, compromise with each other – those kinds of couples will bring their children.

Tears slip down my cheeks. I haven't cried in a long time. With depression pressing down on me for so long, I don't even have the energy to properly cry. My heart hurts. I don't really know why. No, I think I do know why. But it's hard to face it.

Inside my head, another me, a more severe, object-ive me, insists that all of my thoughts about my husband are just paranoia. I half-agree with that. As if making my husband worry for me wasn't enough, now I'm being obses-sive, suspicious and resentful of him with nothing but my own delusions as evidence. What a bitch I am. I really am human trash. I'm the worst . . . When I think like this, my heart calms down. At least this is an emotion I'm familiar with. It's easy to think this is all my fault.

But even if I say it's all my fault and decide to forget everything, there's one thing I can no longer turn back from. The lack of trust I have in my husband. Now that I've con-sidered the possibility of my husband deceiving me, my per-ception of him has changed completely in every regard. The things he's said to me over the last ten years in the name of love. The countless things he's done under the pretext of love. The aggression with which he's treated me in bed. How he removed all kinds of items and relationships from my life, saying that he'd help me cut out things that were unnecessary and harmful. How he completely took away alcohol, cigarettes and social media from me, saying that he'd cure my unhealthy dependence on them. How he took away the month's supply of medication l received from the neuropsychiatrist, saying he was worried I'd abuse it, and doled it out to me day by day like he was feeding kibble to his pet dog. And how he even moved us to this barren plain where there's not a single person l know. All of these things now have different meanings. Once l recognise those meanings, l cannot forget them. l don't know how much is real and how much is fiction. l don't know what l can trust and what l shouldn't. l don't even know what is pain and what is happiness.

l cry for a long time. The snow soaks in all of the sound, so it seems quieter than usual.

Around sunset, l go back into the living room and shut the balcony door. Then l approach the kitchen shelf that holds the medicine bottles. Like salt and pepper shakers, the plastic morning medicine and evening medicine bottles are placed side by side. l dump out the pills from those bottles into my hand.

Then l go to the bathroom and flush them down the toilet.


## 8. The Hallway

My husband is angry with me. He is standing in the hallway outside the dressing room, banging on the wall and shouting at me as l stand inside.

'. . . happen to my reputation?!'

As I remove my stockings, my husband's words go in one ear and out the other. I take off my pearl earrings and put them on top of the dresser. I unfasten my wristwatch. I don't really understand what my husband is saying. These days, I find it difficult to divide my attention between different tasks. It has been three days since I stopped taking my medicine; I feel distracted and seem to have lost the ability to concentrate.

'Did you see Professor Cha's face? Did you see what the other people's faces were like? The new writers there were staring and whispering right in front of us. Do you feel better now after making a fool of yourself?'

Who is Professor Cha again? And the new writers . . . Slowly, as I remove my tweed jacket and skirt and change into a housedress, I turn over my memories. The place I've just come from. A hotel ballroom in the city. A wide hall with round tables, where people dressed in formalwear sipped tea and champagne while exchanging pleasantries.

That's right. I went to an event with my husband today. It was a ceremony for some big literary award. As usual, I wore an elegant outfit chosen by my husband and, with an elaborately made-up face, followed behind him, smiling and greeting this person and that. Most were people I'd met somewhere but couldn't remember the names of. That wasn't a big problem in any case, because I didn't have to converse at length with any of them. Despite my standing right in front of them, the men directed questions about me to my husband. In general, the women glanced at me with a peculiar expression and kept their distance; if they were older, they often said things like, 'How lucky for you that you have such an accomplished husband. When are you planning to have children?'

No. Today was different.

As the memory comes back to me, my face flushes once more in shame.

'Aha, look at you turning red. So you do understand what embarrassment is.'

My husband's voice once again fills my ear. I look up at his face. His face is red and splotchy too, and a vein is throbbing in his neck.

'Of course you should be embarrassed. A full-grown adult crying like that in front of others. Like a simple-minded child. Do you know how awkward you made things for everyone? What the hell was that?'

With my head ducked, I say softly, 'You . . . made things awkward for me.'

'What?'

'You made me a – a fool in front of those people first.'

'When did I ever do that?' my husband asks incredulously.

He truly believes he has never done such a thing. But I noticed the others laughing. When Professor Cha, who'd become an editor at the literary journal where I had made my debut, greeted me warmly. When he asked, 'Aren't you writing anything these days? How about publishing something in the issue after this next one?' And when, before I could say anything, my husband responded instead with great courtesy, 'Thank you for the offer, but I'm afraid that will be difficult given my wife's health.'

At that moment, I felt a strange sort of humiliation.

Of course, Professor Cha's words might not have been sincere. He probably wasn't being sincere. That would have just been his way of expressing his goodwill to my husband, rather than to me. Something said more out of courtesy than anything else. But through a sliver in all the gazes of the people pretending not to see me and in all the words they exchanged that circumvented me, this offer had come to me, directly, for the first time in a long time. And before my eyes, before everyone's eyes, my husband snatched that away. For two or three seconds a small smile flitted across the lips of everyone who'd witnessed the scene and then vanished. A smile meaning 'There you go, then', 'Just as I thought, that woman's not in her right mind.'

Maybe in the past I would have let it happen to me. But this time, I was angry. I couldn't hold back.

'No, I can do it,' I said to Professor Cha, looking him straight in the eye, and everyone grew quiet. Professor Cha looked flustered.

My husband turned it into a joke with the easy manner peculiar to someone who still believed he could control the situation. 'Don't tell me you plan on spilling your past again and then squirming under the covers at night when you feel embarrassed? I don't think I can handle much more of that.'

There was a rather sexual nuance to his words. Professor Cha chuckled and returned the joke with another and showed signs of trying to smooth over the situation. But I had no intention of leaving it like that.

'Whether I choose to spill my past or not is up to me. And I can answer for myself. Let *me* handle whether I take on something or turn it down. Whether I write or don't write. For god's sake, just let me handle it!'

Caught up in the emotions surging through me, I burst into tears. That's right. Just as my husband said, I started crying in front of everyone. Like I wasn't a grown adult. Like I wasn't *normal*. My unexpected outburst made everyone uncomfortable. The men cleared their throats, not knowing what to do. A couple of women whom I didn't recognise handed me some tissues and tried to change the subject. My husband's face was turning bright red.

But I wasn't ashamed. If I could have yelled louder, I would have. I wanted to lay bare everything in my heart as I wailed. That the person who had just shrunk my past into a joke in front of everyone was none other than my husband. That, in those days, he'd been the person I'd loved more than anything, anyone, in the world.

But now, I have no strength to tell this to my husband. Just going over it in my head, I am hit with a wave of exhaustion. I just want to sleep.

'That's enough. I have nothing else to say. I'm tired.'

I give up trying to explain to my husband and step out of the dressing room. He's furious, but I move to brush past him and head silently down the hallway when, suddenly, he swings his hand in the air over my head.

Shocked, I look up into my husband's eyes.

My husband looks down into my eyes.

In that moment, I feel something small yet secure linking the two of us snap. Finally, I understand what I've never understood for the past ten years. Or perhaps what I've come to understand slowly over the past ten years at long last materialises into something I can see and touch. I stare into my husband's bare, vulnerable face. My husband stares into my primal horror. In this space where both of us have become pathetic and insignificant, no words are necessary.

I'm using too much figurative language again.

## 9. The House Opposite

My husband has gone out. I thought he was going for a smoke, but it's been thirty minutes and he still has not come back. I am hovering in the living room, wondering what I'm supposed to do from now on. Just as I'm thinking this, I hear the elevator.

My husband must be coming back.

No, not my husband – it could be the woman in the purple dress.

Or the two of them could be together.

For a moment, I stay still and gather my bearings. Instinctively I search for something to lean on. My eyes fall on the tablet embedded in the living room wall. Suddenly I remember what my husband said – that I can use the tablet to see what's happening right outside the front door in real time, that I can record what's happening too.

I hurry to the tablet, activate the CCTV screen for the outside of the front door and press the record button like my husband taught me. Then I run to the front door and fling it open. Whatever comes out of the elevator, I'm ready to face it. The camera will show proof of that.

The elevator stops on the nineteenth floor. I stand right in front of it. The sliding doors slowly open and one person steps out.

It is the woman in the purple dress.

As she steps out of the elevator, she sees me and halts. I stare blankly at her. She tilts her head, gazing at me. She doesn't know me, but I know her very well. Finally, I remember who she is.

'Can I help you?' the woman asks.

Hurriedly, I blurt out, 'Oh, um, I was curious about something. We're neighbours, you know, and I've seen you around sometimes, and, so . . . Well, I wanted to ask you something. So I thought maybe I'd run into you sometime.'

'I see . . . Please, go ahead.'

With a cautious look on her face, the woman purses her lips. I see the motley shades of make-up applied awkwardly to her face. I see rose-gold-plated earrings that look like they might have been bought at a mechanical parts shop. And I see the dress. The neckline cuts straight over the chest and the shoulder straps extend toward the collarbone and neck, accentuating the lines of the shoulder and chest. The hemline of the dress, which resembles a wrap skirt with a deep slit, extends down in an elegant curve, stopping just above the ankles. Up close, the purple silk shimmers like an iris, with both a darker violet and a brilliant pink colour, depending on the angle of the light that hits it. It doesn't take more than a glance to know it is an expensive dress. In contrast, the woman's arms are bare of any accessories. Her shoes are black, four-centimetre-high heels appropriate for wearing to interviews, and do not go with the dress at all.

'It's just, your dress is so pretty. I was curious where you bought it.'

The woman immediately relaxes and her face brightens.

'Oh, this? I bought it at a vintage shop. It's a real designer dress, but it's kind of old so they sold it for cheap.' She seems to think for a moment and then adds, 'So you can't get it in normal stores anymore. I'm sorry I couldn't be of more help . . .'

'Oh, not at all. Still, it looks expensive. It must have cost a lot of money.'

'I might've overdone it a little.'

The woman grins at me. She doesn't know yet about the rumours spreading on campus that she buys her clothes and purses with the money she gets from her sugar daddy. She doesn't know yet that in just one year she will rush to get rid of this dress for a much lower price because she needs the money. And she doesn't even know that she will completely forget that she ever once owned such a dress. All of that is too far into the future.

'Still, I really wanted to buy it,' the woman adds.

'It's not something you can easily wear day-to-day . . .'

'I don't go out in this dress. This is what I wear when I write. I actually write fiction. There was this famous writer who once said she only feels inspired when she writes in a wedding dress. It was like a weird quirk of hers. So I got myself a little work outfit too. It's my work, after all, I should be able to invest at least this much.'

I nod. That's a very reasonable explanation.

'So are you still writing these days?'

Her face flushing with greater excitement and, at the same time, a touch of embarrassment, the woman clasps her hands together.

'This is a secret but . . . Um . . . If you have some time, would you like to read it? It's still a first draft so there's a lot that needs editing, but . . . if you come over to my place, I can show you.'

The woman motions toward her front door.

It hurts to see how easily she invites strangers into her home. It hurts to know how easily she trusts and likes and loves others. I'm sorry for the relationships she'll develop in the future. But maybe that's just me. She might feel different. This woman may value something else, something I've never thought about.

'Sure. I have lots of time. Is it a novel? Short story? What's it about?'

The woman looks around the dark, empty hallway. Then she brings her lips to my ear and whispers, 'It's a story about a woman who kills her husband.'

## 10. The Kitchen

I step inside my open front door. The motion-sensing light turns on and the interior is coloured with an orangey light. Looking down, I see my husband's slippers lying askew. A faint light and sounds of washing drift from the bathroom.

I approach the tablet embedded in our living room wall.

The video is still recording. I press the stop button and rewatch the footage recorded so far. Only after I watch to the end do I realise that I did not have to watch it at all. I delete the video. Just as I thought, technology like this is useless.

I go to the kitchen and open the base cabinet. There is a compartment inside the cabinet that holds all sorts of knives. A large meat cleaver. A medium-size knife typically for slicing kimchi or other vegetables. A bread knife with its bumpy sawtooth edge. Even a small, light fruit knife. I choose a sharp-edged meat cleaver that I haven't used once since moving, and push to close the compartment. This house certainly is something unique, with its state-of-the-art design. The kitchen seems to be constructed in a way to suit the user's convenience. The drawers and cabinets move slickly without a sound and put everything that's necessary within reach. I dampen a new rag I got from some window-blind-installation company that was stuck within a promotional flyer. Sure enough, the rag has the words *Congratulations on your move!* on it.

In this newly built apartment complex, in this new city, everyone is optimistic about the future. That life in general will be easier here. That our everyday lives will be changed. That we'll be so much happier than before. And they try their hardest to instil in you that same confidence. Ultimately, my husband was right. Once anyone has lived in a new apartment, they'll wonder how they ever managed to live in the old one.

I take the knife and the rag and head to the bathroom.

I plan on cleaning it thoroughly today.

# Montage

I am going to you.

I don't know your name. You don't have a name. But everyone thinks of you. Each of us has our own name for you. Genius. Recluse. Hope. Salvation. Initials from A to Z. We want to call you something. We want to turn your blurred silhouette into something we can hold in our hands. Each of us wants to grant you a title we think is most fitting for you. That you rejected a name makes us even more anxious. We want to elevate you to be in history books, literature books, in places that award famous literary prizes. But your physical self won't ever stand on such a stage, will it? At an empty venue after the host speaks your name, we want to spill our tears into the noble silence that follows, the void that is restored, as we praise your virtue.

You may regard our worldly concerns with pity. We who are average citizens. Who prostrate ourselves at the feet of a world bursting with proper nouns. Who lick our lips at the thought of dragging you into such a world. I don't deny that I, too, am such a person. But I'd like to maintain that at least my purpose in seeking you out is not like the others'. I'd like to maintain that my intentions in seeking you out are a bit more pure, a bit more innocent, than the others'. But I know this desire of mine doesn't make the slightest difference. I know that even just attaching the words 'a bit more' to 'pure' and 'innocent' makes it no longer pure, no longer innocent. Even so, I sincerely hope you'll understand me for having no choice but to go looking for you.

I hope you will understand my begging for your language.

I am driving at the moment. The car has made it through the city's bustling morning rush hour and is heading down the highway. You've probably ridden in a car like this one, haven't you? Though probably not in the driver's seat like me. You've probably also seen the scene I now see outside the car window, haven't you? Though your attention at the time would've likely been focused on the seat next to you, not out the window. At least that's what I'm assuming. I follow your path of movement as best I can. Believing that if I keep following the path you followed, if I see what you saw, experience what you experienced, eventually I'll be able to see you.

Of course, I may fail again. I've already failed three times so to fail once more wouldn't be unheard of. Plenty of people apart from me have tried to find you and no one has succeeded yet. Because you are a notorious recluse. Your novels turn up on their own, out of the blue, with no sign or hint as to where they came from or where they're going. When the news breaks that a novel with only a title has dropped, people race to the bookstores. Once they're done singing your praises, inevitably they want to find you.

Whenever a new journalist joins any kind of newspaper, magazine or TV broadcast station, they throw themselves

into looking for you, almost like a rite of passage. Your
fans have made an online fan page for you and write you
letters without any idea whether or not you, their idol, are
a member of the site. Aspiring writers who dream of being
like you poke around publishing houses, literary circles and
schools, hoping to be your mentee. But you are nowhere.
No matter the commotion we make, we receive not a single
reaction from you. In the span of time that your three books
were published, there was never any sign of you. People
came up with, and dismissed, countless theories about you.
They speculated that your reclusiveness was just a market-
ing ploy. Or that you were a famous writer already, staying
anonymous to play a joke on us. After your second book
came out, there was a hypothesis that you were an unmen-
tionable figure whose identity was never to be divulged.
After your third book came out, some people proposed
that you were actually a collective of several lesser-known
writers. But whether you are one or many is not important.
Because you exist only in the empty margins, and empty
margins cannot be counted. Only your language can.

Your stories are special. Somehow, some way, people
want to define your specialness, so they use the old-
fashioned term 'hard-boiled'. Even though it's incorrect. The
detectives in your stories and the words you use to make
those detectives move never professed to be level-headed
or objective. Stepping back and abandoning judgement is
a flavour of cowardice that doesn't suit you. Your cases are
not about spelling out that life is dark and irrational. No,
rather, your stories slice precisely through the darkness and
the irrationality, like the beam of oncoming headlights. But

it would be a misnomer to call the light 'truth'. Because you know well that the truth is the darkness itself. The moment you illuminate us, our truth vanishes in a flash and in its place only your light remains, defining our shape and contours. Life is always one step behind your words. For example, even my decision to go looking for you happened a long time after your words. That's right, I'm the same as the rest.

I'm sure that I'm the first reader to confess her love to you, just like every reader is sure they're the first too. When I read a short piece of your writing for the first time, I was first shocked by your arrogance, then I felt my heart burn as though scalded. You spoke about everything, just as it was. Everything except for death. About everyone's goodness and love, in spite of their sins and vices, their truths and lies, and things that belong in none of those categories. About everyone living lives as victims, culprits and detectives all at once. And ultimately you imposed order upon our chaos and returned all that had been scattered back to its proper place. No, I should say, there never existed a proper place: it came to be through you. You spoke of hope and only then did people hope. Only because of your stories did people examine their lives. They cradled the precious, fragrant hope given freely to them and did not doubt that it was their very own special hope. That's right. I'm not surprised that they think of your fiction as their own personal story. Anyone might discover themselves in your work. People said, 'It's like this writer saw right into my mind.' 'This is exactly my life.'

And, yes, I was the same at first. It was like everything I wanted to forget, everything I wanted to deny, everything I didn't want to remember, was contextualised in your writing. And that seemed to reconstruct my own experiences. You spoke like you knew me better than I did myself. You spoke like you remembered the moments I didn't remember and forgot the moments I couldn't forget. I couldn't help but urge you to reveal them. Like an amnesiac discovering a diary in their old home, I followed along, face flushed in a kind of vulgar way. But at the last moment, I was betrayed. I closed your books shut. My excitement crumbled. There were none of my sins, my vices, my virtues, nor the love I gave and received. I could find none of it. I only discovered my pathetic, lonely body, exhilarated and panting with a useless longing to be whole, to have hope, through your language. How could I not have loved your beautiful, vast language that was the exact inverse of me?

How can I not think of your books as 'my story'? How can your brilliant prose, your precise technique, your concrete descriptions, not clothe me perfectly? Every time I drown in the crest of emotion you've put down on paper, every time I agree with your characters, why do I feel like a thief stealing a relic from a church? Why am I still here in the end, unable to call your name, stubbornly dragging my lumbering body to put my hands on the steering wheel? This is probably my fault. It can't be yours. Because you did your best to deliver your language to us in its entirety. Because you did everything you could to make your writing into something merely written, something like dust scattered in the wind, something that would not corrode or diminish even though anyone could declare it theirs. I can't imagine how intensely you must have struggled to pull that off. I don't dare fathom how you were able to erase yourself so thoroughly. I don't want to betray your pristine efforts. Never. I hope more than anyone that your labour will reach me and come to fruition. Some shameless critic dared to go through your works and categorise them, predicting how you'd grown up, your social status, age, background and occupation, like some fake fortune-teller. I ground my teeth watching this. I truly have no interest in any of that. That is not why I'm looking for you.

I'm just curious. About why you wanted to disappear that badly. And why I – why I alone – am not permitted to fill your vacant seat.

The car is passing through a small coastal city. Motels and hwe restaurants – now in their off-season – inscribe the air with their fluorescent-coloured signs, letters missing in places. The groan of waves swallowing discarded items. The sound of dogs barking. I imagine you sitting in the back seat and listening to these noises. I imagine you not speaking but listening. I imagine your silence that I wouldn't be able to hear when you're speaking. How peaceful and absolute that silence would be. It'd be as natural as your speech. You use words exactly as decreed by God. You arrange them in a harmonious order, like the changing of the seasons, the flight patterns of migratory birds, the ebb and flow of the tides. And I think of the countless people who have matched their life's order with your order. And of the people who, from your vacant seat, scrape together your words like flakes of panned gold and pass them down to others. Among them, some will use your absence to seize ownership of your words. And even though you've not designated an heir, there will be a never-ending stream of people who consider themselves your rightful successor. You'd maintain your silence even in the face of such an invasion, such an insult, wouldn't you? An absolute, thus powerless, silence.

I am completely different from you. I always have been. I never wanted to disappear. If anything, I always wanted my existence to be known. I didn't want to die without a sound, alone somewhere and without anyone knowing. Can you even understand how desperate a longing that was? Can you imagine what it's like for someone to live with a gag in her mouth? Can you fathom the sensation of being buried with your mouth blocked shut? How much, up to what point, and exactly how far, could you imagine and write a silence that, unlike yours, was imperfect? A silence with holes here and there, that was burning and hideously swollen, that fought and wavered and surrendered and screamed? I was deeply curious. This is the murder that took place in your first novel.

Your story began on the night of a bright full moon that bathed the earth in silver. In a field thick with weeds, as a crisp autumn wind passed through the trees and the crickets and frogs and other unknown insects sang in unison, you showed us a victim who'd been raped and murdered. You told us how the victim had been kidnapped; how they'd been dragged away; how the body had been deprived of its freedom; how the body had been injured and invaded; how, ultimately, it had lost its life; and that part of the dead body had been washed away so it might never be identified. The description was extremely graphic, but since it omitted all details about the victim's body or any personal backstory related to their state of mind, you could read it as every rape and murder that had ever happened in the world. The victim in that story wasn't the wreckage of something that had once been a human. It was only seen as the physical evidence of human violence.

Please don't misunderstand. I don't think your way is wrong. Some people have criticised you for your display of senseless cruelty, but not me. Because I've experienced it. I experienced it . . . When someone's hands are pressed against our mouths, when our bodies are weighed down and our legs twist so we can't move, when things happen to our bodies against our will and we can't say one word, let alone what we think – we can't be called people. While that's happening, we aren't alive. We, I, didn't consider myself alive at the time. My mind left my body and hovered in mid-air; my body existed at every other time except for the present; and my emotions stopped responding to all stimuli. I . . . can't call that anything but death. I'd already died once at the time. And . . . I don't know anything about myself from back then. I only remember how bright the moon was that night, how softly everything around me gleamed silver. I don't remember the wind on my skin, but I remember the curve of the ripples it made as it swept through the grass. I don't remember the sound of my body being destroyed, but I remember the cries of insects getting

188

higher and lower in pitch as though they'd divided up their song by vocal range. And . . .

You wouldn't have been able to tell your story any other way. Truly, there is no better way. There is no approach better than death . . . Because at the time I wished I were actually dead. Because the death I experienced then – even death, just like all of my other experiences – was imperfect. Even then I couldn't forget my body. I can never forget how cumbersome it is. For a long time after, I couldn't help but be constantly aware of my body. I didn't want to be ashamed but my body constantly reminded me of its humiliation. I just wanted to become lighter. Piece by piece, I wanted to cut off the flesh hanging from my frame. I wanted to slice through my vocal cords that wanted to say that I was in pain, that I wanted to live, that I wanted to tear off my gag and scream, that I wanted to crawl out of the deep, cold earth. The only thing that was clear to me was . . . wanting to disappear . . . Wanting to disappear alone somewhere and without anyone knowing was my most significant desire, and it felt like you had finally made it happen. Only in your story.

I beg you, please notice my silence. I who have been forsaken outside of your story. Please notice my worn-down face every time you speak.

You don't know how earnestly I've wanted to talk about what I went through. It felt impossible to carry around everything that was bubbling in my throat. I wanted to explain to people why my body was imperfect, why there were holes here and there, why it goes around in its burned and hideously swollen state – and beg their forgiveness. No, that's not it. I wanted to confess to the people who thought I was like them that, actually, I had a body that had holes in it here and there, that it was burned and hideously swollen – and beg their forgiveness. Because as long as I didn't do that I would never be able to forgive myself. But, ah, what will I be able to say about what happened? What should I say it was, how should I define it? Whatever cause and effect I try to grant it, whatever linearity, whatever role and relationship, all of it seems inadequate. All the words that come out of my mouth are completely wrong; they're crooked and maimed. I can't use these sloppy and mediocre words to pull my sloppy and mediocre self together.

But you, you alone, can speak of it flawlessly. Your words will be able to explain me. They'll be able to piece together my irremediable body; they'll define my shape and contours; they'll make me into something that has a texture you can feel and an exterior you can see. They'll be able to explain to me precisely what my experience was, how I'm supposed to accept it, how I'm supposed to deal with it. Through your lips I'll become something that I'll be able to understand, that others will be able to understand too. If only I could find you. If only I could find you somewhere and clutch your wrist and have my name called by you. If only I could do that . . .

Before long, the sky grows dark outside the car window. I am driving along the brightly lit national highway, my foot on the accelerator. On either side of the highway there are identical container depots; every now and then I see a vehicle unloading freight. Soon we'll be in the middle of nowhere. With only bleak farmlands that people pretended to grow crops on in order to avoid taxes and mountain peaks with abandoned graves amidst their vegetation. I know this route well, because it was the setting of your second novel.

I remember the man in your novel quite well too. He was healthy, brimming with vigour. And he was arrogant. His arrogance was completely different from yours. He believed he could speak on everything; he even believed he could speak on death. Since he'd rightfully inherited your flawless language, he believed he could show off his authority anywhere and exercise his power toward anyone. He didn't seem to have a single shred of doubt about this. I couldn't help but be drawn to his assuredness. I wondered if such a man's authority might liberate me. Of course, I was restrained at that time too. My body, which hadn't been free for a long time, was like a wild animal trapped in a cage – I was innocent, though unhappy, and got angry for no reason. I babbled in excitement, indiscriminately, to anyone that fed me. My body was one among many mysteries that my inadequate language could not distinguish, but unlike other mysteries it terrified me because it controlled my very desire to speak. So I could do nothing but bind my body tighter than ever so it wouldn't break free. While I was like this, you suddenly strode toward me. And as I kept smiling and listening to your words, nodding my head, you said you liked me. Me, nodding while tied up. Right, well, maybe he'll teach me how to speak. I think that's what I thought. Or, actually, maybe I thought he'll teach me how to be whole in the silence. I don't know. I still don't. Maybe such stupidity was my fault.

I know. You didn't say it was my fault. You never started your stories intending to criticise me. You would've only wanted to explain why I agreed to get into his car, why I made no sound even as I was pulled toward a darkness in the middle of nowhere. You would've only wanted to explain why I got out of the car and followed him into the quiet field and lay under him. Why I had no choice but to do so. But to me, your explanation was . . . I washed my hands over and over. My menstrual bleeding lasted an entire month. I washed my body for three hours. I wasn't able to walk properly. Because the flowers and dog faeces and fruits that had festered and burst looked so disgusting to me I couldn't bear it. The world around me was unbe- lievably foul. Also you . . . When I was finally released from my long imprisonment, I was already in his car and only he existed beside me. My body had been flailing in every dir- ection, not knowing what to do, and that's what he'd sug- gested to me. How could I have done anything different? So I made the choice to—But wait, was that really my choice? In a world where the only options that exist are 'yes' or 'no', in a world where the only options given to me are to get in someone's car that will take me somewhere or to get out of the car and be left in the dark, the only choice I can make is . . . But is that really what you think? That was the only possibility?

Of course, you probably couldn't help but think that. Because only then are you able to speak. You never wanted to return to the darkness of before so you thought to rely on his deceptive authority, in a false hope that he would take me somewhere vast, clean and gleaming. So you believed I loved him, that it was an act of love – no, that's what you wanted to believe – so I would've said yes. But that's a lie. In reality, I didn't say anything at all. Everything happened in silence. And what you thought were my feelings of love were in the end nothing but delusion that my own inherent lack might be love. Anticipation that it might become love. Shame toward my inability to know what love is. Incoherence that doesn't even let me feel pain . . . Oh, it's no use trying to take back your mistake and offer explanations now. You still don't know? Your ludicrous arrogance is exactly like that man's. You might not want to believe it, but it's the truth. You got here by collecting the dregs of authority leaked by that man, by stealing the car he drives, by imitating his words. But no matter how hard I try to inch that damned car forward, shine my headlights and search every bit of the ground where I'm buried for traces of me, all of my truth only recedes into the darkness.

You know. You know, don't you? People don't forgive me. They never accept my hideous body with holes here and there, a body that was burned and swollen. No matter how noble the words you used were – or, no, perhaps because of them – the moment I appear before you, people will scramble to be the first to stone me in their horror. I'm saying you deceived them. You used those rightful heirs' words, stolen from their church, for evil and vulgar purposes. With my appearance alone, all of your words become a horrible fabrication. They become gibberish not worth listening to. Newspapers, magazines and TV stations will all thrust their cameras into your face, your fans will rip up your books or light them on fire, aspiring writers will begin making fun of you. Some people will never believe it. That all those words were written for a person like me – someone as pathetic as me. That all of that writing was an attempt to explain my life, to defend my experience, to make me into something that could be understood. The fact that, ultimately, their lives aren't much different from mine. The fact that to receive hope while there was no order, no 'proper place' in their lives – lives made up of delusion, anticipation, shame, incoherence – they had to pay a tremendous price. The people who refuse to believe those facts will ridicule me and trample me. And the people who realise those facts will probably want to kill me. Because if I didn't exist, they can be right. Because of that . . . I am walking, mute, left behind in the darkness in the wake of your dazzling light. Even if all the words that came after 'yes' betrayed me. Even though you changed my name, hollowed out my emotions, reversed the chronology. Even though you told my story in its entirety to people who are most definitely not me and alienated me in their favour. I am behind you. Always behind you.

I pull over to the hard shoulder and think of you. I gaze at the glow from the headlights spilling across the asphalt and the fields blanketed in darkness and think of you. I lean my forehead against the steering wheel and think of your name. Because I want to call out to you. Because I want to grab hold of you and for once – just once – make you turn around to look at me. Only then can I be certain. That there must have been a time before you left this unbridgeable distance between us. A time before I slipped into the darkness, before you betrayed me . . . Do you remember the silence that surrounded us back then? Do you remember what you said in that silence that was neither 'yes' nor 'no'? I don't. I don't even remember your name. I can't call out to you even though I so desperately want to. The more I say something, the more I lose my grasp of it. The more anxiously I call out for something, the fewer traces I find of it.

I remember the last time I said your name. I remember it so vividly. It was a Wednesday. We were in the car with our parents. Father was in the driver's seat. Mother in the passenger seat. We were side by side in the back. You were on the right and I was on the left, to be exact. It was a holiday and we were heading toward Father's parents' house. Our car set out early in the morning, passed through a long, congested stretch of road, stopped by a coastal city, wound through the city streets and then got back on the national highway. During those three hours, Mother and Father didn't say a single word to each other. Probably because we were there. If they absolutely had to say something to each other they just said it through us. Like, 'Sweetie, go to the restroom with your dad.' Or 'Your mum said she forgot to pack that toy. She was distracted.' Their silences were as different as their manner of speech. Father's silence was heavy and oppressive. Mother's silence trickled downward and pooled onto the floor of the car. We were afraid of our mother's silence because we couldn't understand it. We took Father's silence as a sign that as long as we didn't disobey him everything would be fine. But we had no way to protect ourselves from our mother's silence, which lapped at our ankles and kept rising higher and higher. So you began to speak. You started telling me things non-stop. Fun stories, scary stories, surprising stories, strange stories . . . Eventually the sky outside the car window grew dark and the surface of the road glowed red. There were container depots lined up on either side of the highway and men loading and unloading cargo in front of the trucks, but you didn't pay attention to that. You were busy telling stories. Mother's silence was already up to your waist. I was fully engrossed in listening and laughing and admiring your stories, eating snacks, dozing off, pointing at something outside the window. I was truly happy listening to all those stories . . . You didn't sleep at all the whole time we were in the car. Because you weren't sure if the silence would reach your head and swallow you whole while you were snoring away. So you kept saying things . . . But what did you say? What were you talking about? I remember every-thing else so vividly, but not that. I remember the hap-piness and peace I felt then, but not anything you talked about . . . As the bleak farmlands and the small, secluded mountain peaks stretched on outside the car window, night fell. The moon was in the sky. There wasn't a single other car on the road. Father drove on without stopping. His face growing stonier. You wanted to ask where we were, where Grandma's house was, how much longer until we got there, but you couldn't. Father kept on driving into the night, the pitch-black night, and it didn't seem like we were driving, but rather being pulled into it; and Mother's silence continued to rise . . . You kept talking, not even knowing what you were talking about, and while you went on and on . . . you needed to squeeze out every single word you knew, and right when your tongue dried up with anxiety about what to do if you used up your last words . . . Father stopped the car. He stopped the car and then turned back to look at you.

I remember the surge of terror that went through us at that moment. Thinking back on it now, I think that terror has been with me since I was born. Father's face contorted in rage. His real features were nowhere to be found. No, maybe to me Father's face had always been contorted like that. Father said to you that you shouldn't say things like that. What was he talking about? He said all your stories were wrong. What stories were those? We were ashamed without even knowing why. You said to Father, 'No. That's not it.' You said again, 'No.' And then Father told you to get out of the car.

Everyone knew what getting out of the car meant. But Mother didn't stop Father and I wasn't able to hold you back. I remember you looking back at the open car door with fear in your eyes. I remember Father seizing your arm and dragging you away. You pleaded over and over again, I was wrong, I'm sorry, I was wrong, I'm sorry, but it was no use. Because Father already knew you were lying. All of us knew it. The red hazard lights shone over your feet as you were dragged away, whimpering, as you were raked against the asphalt. Father's grip was strong and you were nearly frozen with terror but you did your best to fight him off. But before your eyes you could see the guardrail along the

hard shoulder and the field beyond it. An abandoned piece
of land thick with weeds, where the clamour of the insects
blended with your screams. I saw you being dragged there
clear as day. Soon after, your screams stopped. And until
your silhouette disappeared into the deep darkness of the
land . . .

I called out your name.

I look around the inside of the unfamiliar car that isn't
mine, that will never be mine. Not at the beam of light
slicing across the darkness outside my window, but at the
things inside the car. At the seats covered in leather according to the tastes of a man I don't know. At the sprinkling of
dirt and scraps of leaves on the seats and the floor. At the
odometer keeping record of distances I didn't drive. The
LCD screen with a blinking Bluetooth icon that I've never
figured out how to connect to. The rotary gear-shift dial
that my hand isn't used to . . . and the passenger seat. The
passenger seat that once seated Mother, then me, and is
now vacant. I leave all of those things bathed in the car's
interior light. I open the door and step out, one foot at a
time, into the blur of darkness. I approach the guardrail and
look out at the field stretching before me.

A place where I can see nothing but darkness. You, in
seclusion, in the darkness. The only genius I know. My
salvation. My hope. I am going through initials from A to
Z. What was your name? What were those stories you told
that day? What happened to you? Did you die? Or were
you buried? Are you screaming with your mouth blocked
shut? Is no one listening as you say you're in pain, you

want to live, you want to crawl out of the earth? Or did you run away? Are you on the run, forever retreating to a place where no one knows you, where no one can call out to you? I've been working so desperately hard. While I was writing my three novels, I thought I was telling those stories for you, you who were somewhere. And everybody said my stories were perfect. They all said they were able to find themselves in my work. But you – you all – remained silent. In the face of your draconian silence, I lost three times and I think I'll keep losing forever. But . . . I remember your stories that surrounded me that day. They were like a sturdy wall and a soft blanket at the same time, so that nothing in the world could invade me. But in the gap between phrases, the gap between words, the changing of the seasons, the flight patterns of migratory birds and the ebb and flow of the tides were clearly visible. How could it be so clear? Your name was mine. And in those days when my name could be yours, the word 'love', the sound of it, the meaning of it, the writing of it, all overlapped each other and fell like snowflakes on my skin. Even though all those snowflakes melted as soon as Father dragged you away . . . But I – I remember. That that was never a lie to be ashamed of. Because you were holding me before I could tell innocence and deception apart; your body temperature was your words and I was there to hear them. Reflecting on the warm, firm grip you had on my hand, I think of how hard you tried to protect me, how desperately you tried to swallow your fear and keep talking as days and years went by. So . . .

I'm going to keep fighting too. No matter how rough my

words are, even if they're completely stolen, even if they're all forgotten someday . . . If I could only see you, even for just a moment, and press my lips to you.

So now I'm calling out to you. Even if calling you without a name doesn't help me get to you at all. Even though it scares me that if I do this I might lose you forever. I'm calling out to you.

I lean my arms against the guardrail and gaze at the field. Now adjusted to the darkness, my eyes catch the fine shadows cast by the bushes in the moonlight. And the furrows made by the crisp wind as it sweeps through the grass as if showing off its shape and contours. And between those furrows I hear countless crickets and frogs and other unknown insects moving about. When I close my eyes and open them, between those thick bushes, in the darkness over there, I think I can see your hair fluttering in the wind. The shoes in your hand sway in time to your limping footsteps.

# The Sacrifice

# I.

Just as no one remembered when the island came to exist, no one remembered when the shrine on the island was built. Why, how, and by whom was it constructed? No records remained. Only that the shrine was there before they were born and it would remain there after they died, like it had been part of the island's geology from the very beginning. No different from a cave or a valley or a volcano.

The island was not far. When the weather was clear, the island stood out vividly from its spot on the horizon, easily visible from anywhere in the village. It looked like a tree stump chopped by a skilled woodcutter. Lying low and flat, the disc-shaped rocky island was completely deserted except for a dark, wooden building. With the island itself being a sort of foundation stone, at first glance the shrine looked like it was floating by itself on the sea. It gave that impression even more so on days when it was cloudy or the fog upon the sea was thick. In the fog rolling across the surface of the water, the island's contours were hidden; only the outline of the shrine's roof and gabled walls bobbed unexpectedly through the air. Some people claimed the shrine actually moved little by little, following the tides. Even if that were the case, the location of the island did not shift within their world, rather their world shifted with the location of the island; thus, it wasn't something humans had the power to measure. No different from the movement of continents or glaciers or the North Star.

The people of the village served the god at the shrine. They knew the god to be a massive sea serpent who calmed the waves, guided boats and governed their haul of fish. According to legend, the serpent was a divine beast, large enough to swallow five boats at once, with a back that was red like refined copper, a stomach the colour of ivory and eyes the colour of amber. A single blow of his tail made the waves rise and a single bat of his fin made the winds blow. With one pointed fang he could save fish that were dying; with the other he could kill fish that were alive.

This divine serpent who ruled the seas was not, by nature, kind to humans. Boats that launched without his permission were drawn into the tongue of his waves, chewed up with the teeth of his reef, and smashed to pieces. Everyone believed that the reason their husbands and sons were able to catch an abundance of hardy fish every season, sell them shoreside and then safely return home was thanks to the rituals they faithfully performed for the sea serpent. They saw no reason to test the god's fury by ceasing them.

The village had a long tradition of offering a young girl to the sea serpent. Because the sea serpent only consumed maidens of marriageable age, there was no use in offering a beast or a man or a child or someone elderly. And so the men would journey to foreign lands and visit the poorest households; and when they'd return with a newborn baby girl, the women would take turns caring for her, raising her with love until she was sixteen. As if the men had brought back food from the market and the women were preparing it in the kitchen. The maiden who was to be the offering had to be sold to them at such a young age that she would never think to doubt, much less oppose, her fate. She must be pure. She must bear no cracks in either her mind or her body. She must be more beautiful and more virtuous than anyone else. She would be a rare soul who was more than worthy to be the bride of a god and as such she'd be entitled to be treated with grace. The village elders would teach the maiden this, just as they had learned from their parents; everyone else in the village would follow these teachings too, and thus raise the girl.

Out of their freshly caught seafood, only the fattest cod, the crab bearing the most eggs, and the horse mackerel that gleamed the brightest blue went to the maiden. Even from their land yields, only rice from the glossiest crop, tender ribs of a heifer and richly sweet plums and straw-berries and pears graced the maiden's table. The maiden wore clothes woven from the softest silk, and bathed in the cleanest water infused with the most fragrant flowers and tree bark. And even though she had the prettiest of dolls, of ssamji to carry her coins, of daenggi decorating her braid, of garakji on her finger, if she happened to get bored of them and throw them away, no one would scold her. The maiden was so accustomed to luxuries other girls wouldn't dare dream of that it didn't even occur to her to act conceited. A woman became corrupted when she began to discern between vanity and modesty, and so the maiden, who was to remain pure, was never allowed to hold a brush or turn the page of a book.

There were many other things that were forbidden to her. She was not to get hurt or associate with men. Her body was not her own or her parents', it was the god's, so she was to be careful of her conduct and avoid anything that might defile her. She was not to leave her home without her maid. She was not to leave the village under any circumstances. She was to live her life only in the village and die only at the shrine on the island. While the other women sat atop rocks that had been baking in the scorching sun, their skin burning and their hands chafing from straw and brine as they strung up pollack to dry, the maiden shaded her face with golden hemp and walked delicately, crushing lugworms with feet shod in floral-patterned kkotsin, pale white fingers clutching her skirt. While girls frolicked through the sand and the pine forest and visited this house and that, roughhousing like puppies with the boys until they fell asleep, the maiden remained ensconced in a secret room like a jewellery box, surrounded by stone walls, doing embroidery all day long.

The whole village monitored her. She knew nothing of the world beyond; and even if some outside affair caught her ears, it was only imaginary. A rumour. An old story. In reality, the only freedom the maiden was allowed was deciding what to embroider upon her cloth. She sat where the sunlight was the brightest – in front of a window that showed her nothing but the ocean and the island – and, with her embroidery hoop and the generous amount of silk she'd been provided beside her, she let herself imagine. Green meadows she had never visited. Mountain peaks blanketed in snow. Golden fields of barley that rippled in the breeze. Grand palaces and gardens of the capital. A bustling crowd in the marketplace. The heady fragrance of plum blossoms and water lilies and forsythias and peonies and countless other flowers whose names she did not know. Elephants and monkeys and black-skinned girls from distant foreign lands. The faces of her mother and father. The face of her dear husband whom she could only see in her dreams. With an ink stick she sketched all the images in her head and then used her colourful silk threads atop them to make stitch after careful stitch. Adding layer upon layer of shape and colour, the maiden's world came to life in her embroidery hoop. A wide-open world, but one that was finished at the same time. On her cloth, a crane flew. A magnolia petal fell. A peach started ripening, then spoiled before its time, and was buried in the mud until it once again sprouted. Sometimes she would gaze at her hoop, smiling; other times she would gaze through the window for a long while. The ceaseless crashing of the deep blue ocean echoed throughout her room and drowned out the sound of her dear husband's footsteps. When the Heavenly King of the West wept his summer monsoon season, the maiden thought she wanted to die, then thought, no, she didn't want to die, and cut up her silk embroidery into pieces and burned them in the furnace. That was the biggest act of defiance she could carry out. Because the maiden knew that after she was offered to the god, the village would take all of the embroidery she'd done while she was alive and sell it far and wide, in every country, and then use the money to buy and raise another maiden.

In the spring of the maiden's sixteenth birthday, the village held a pungeoje ritual for the safe and bountiful catch of fish. The households with boats shouldered the cost, while a family that had experienced no misfortune officiated the ritual. The day of the ritual was always clear and the wind still. Like the ocean and sky knew something was about to be offered and were waiting in calm anticipation. Like, if you listened carefully, you could hear the god breathe. The villagers built an altar directly facing the island and the shrine on the horizon. The munyeo then presented alcohol in the direction of the island and danced and sang in praise of the sea serpent until sunset. They prepared a boat decorated with paper flowers and lanterns. The maiden, dressed in clean, white, cotton ceremonial wear and made up prettily with powder and rouge, then approached the altar. For sixteen years, she had been fed and washed and raised for this exact moment; now, clearly blossomed, she looked so beautiful as to appear not of this world. By the time the maiden had climbed into the boat and the skilled boatman had donned his mask and grasped the oar, dusk had fallen and the tide had ebbed to the other side of the coast. Like the island was beckoning the boat to come closer, come closer. Like, along with the water, the light and the sound and the air itself were being drawn to the island. Lamplight flickered like fireflies above the inky ocean depths. The sight of the boat being pulled into the sea looked rather peaceful, as though it were sailing leisurely by the lakeshore. From behind, the maiden, who was seated at the bow wearing a conical white hat, looked like a pale silver moon gliding across the night sky. A moon that would soon be swallowed up by the night. The villagers held their breath as they watched this, overcome with fear as well as with a strange sort of sympathy, wanting the moment to both last forever and end right away. This was the only time any boat touched the island. When they went fishing, they always kept a wide berth from the island; even if the weather was awful and the deck had been destroyed, the boatmen never ever anchored on the island – except for now. The boatman only watched the maiden descend from the boat, walk to the shrine and sit upon its floor, and then made haste to return to the village.

The villagers gathered the ritual materials and went back to their homes. During the long and quiet night, they believed the sea serpent would eat the maiden alive. With the darkness enveloping the horizon, no one would see that spectacle. Once the maiden had stepped foot in the shrine, not a single fragment of her bones would return to them. Some people claimed to hear an odd sound amidst the crash of the waves, like the peal of a bell or someone singing, but no one had ever said they heard screams.

When the new day dawned, the munyeo went to the beach to confirm whether the god was satisfied with their offering and pray for the maiden's soul to live a long life. Then all the villagers held a sumptuous feast where they ate and drank and danced and sang and celebrated the passing of the old and the coming of the new.

The villagers sold every piece of embroidery that the maiden had left behind. They didn't recognise any of the content or the value of her work. Only that merchants always came right on cue to purchase the folding screens and comforters and pouches and norigae at a high price.

Soon, a new child arrived. The village returned to its routine and the island went back to its place.

## 2.

There was a warrior. He was the son of a noble family that had produced generations of brilliant warriors who fought for their country. The warrior grew up straight and honest under his family's pristine upbringing and had a good-natured temper. His inability to distinguish between recklessness and bravery, spirit and self-righteousness, which is so characteristic of youth, was not a flaw but rather a virtue in the warrior. For only such a warrior would be able to save the maiden.

Rumours of the coastal village's religious rites eventually made it to the warrior's ears. Deploring this cruel and indecent custom, the warrior grabbed his bow and quiver of arrows and travelled a great distance until he reached the village. Not only were the villagers unwelcoming of outsiders, but they looked so obviously uncomfortable upon seeing the warrior's bow that he quickly concocted a story, saying he'd merely come in search of a work of embroidery.

'I have lost my treasured gungdae,' he said, referring to the cloth sleeve he used to carry his bow. 'I have come here hearing rumours of an embroidery master living in your village. If I can have a new gungdae made, I will pay any price you ask and be on my way.'

Tempted by his promise to pay anything they asked, the villagers decided to accept the warrior's request. Under the premise of needing to discuss the embroidery project, the warrior obtained the chance to speak with the maiden.

The maiden's boudoir exuded a smell of starch adhesive used on clothing. In one corner, the embroidery hoop, a small wooden chest and colourful boxes woven from bamboo were lined up side by side. The maiden was seated modestly on a cushion, her face obscured by a screen. Only her small white hands could be seen, clasped together, resting on a navy-blue skirt that was finely embroidered with hydrangeas. Seated faithfully next to her was the girl who was both the maiden's attendant and the spy appointed by the villagers to keep an eye on her.

'I fear my skill is lacking, but if my lord sketches the design that was upon the gungdae he lost, if it pleases him, I shall use it as a template.'

The maiden spoke as if to herself. The warrior realised he wouldn't be able to communicate freely with her away from the prying eyes of the village. The maiden hadn't learned how to write so they couldn't exchange written messages. The only thing she understood were shapes and colours on top of textiles; and if it was about them, there was no one who understood better. So the warrior accepted the white silk offered to him by the maiden and, ink stick in hand, drew his design on top. The warrior's drawing depicted a dragon fighting a serpent. The large horned dragon, with the mystical yeouiju orb in its mouth, had the horrible serpent clutched in its talons and was on the verge of tearing the serpent apart.

The dragon symbolised the harmony and the natural balance between the sky, the earth and man. The serpent, on the other hand, was a wicked monster that hid below the sea and consumed virgins to sustain itself. From the beginning, the serpent had only ever been a creature unable to become a dragon; however strong it was, it wasn't a noble god from the legends, only an evil spirit that harassed the people and disturbed the natural order of the world. But, ignorant of this, the people of the village worshipped the evil spirit and kept committing a sin. Hence the warrior had come to defeat the sea serpent, and if the maiden agreed with his intent and offered her help, she would be able to escape her fate.

The warrior was not well versed in calligraphy and painting, so he was not able to express everything he wished to, but he did his best. His sketch was plain and rough like that of a little boy's, for he had no ulterior motive nor any desire to show off; his will was only to right a wrong.

The maiden received the warrior's drawing through her attendant. For a long while, the maiden's hand, gripping the ink-splashed silk, did not move.

At the end of the silence, the maiden spoke. 'It will take time for this embroidery to be completed. To suitably adorn a gungdae worthy of carrying my lord's bow, it will take no less than one thousand winters. But the time I have is far less; for that I am deeply regretful. Next year, on the first full moon of spring, I will forever be departing this life on land. If my lord will return to me on that day, I will do all that I can to have everything prepared.'

The warrior understood the maiden's meaning and was

reassured that his intent had been conveyed. He promised the maiden to do as she asked and left the village.

A year passed, and on the night of the first full moon of spring the warrior returned to the village. With the munyeo's singing and the jangling of her beads, the ritual seemed to be reaching its climax; in its midst, one man greeted the warrior at the outskirts of the village. He ushered the warrior into an empty house and pulled out a mask from the folds of his hanbok. The gaksital, bulging with spots of rouge on its cheeks and thickly arched brows like the face of a bride, was so old that its colours were completely faded.

'I am the boatman who was supposed to row the young lady to the island today. Since men are not to step foot there, we boatmen always don this gaksital to avoid the wrath of the god. Change clothes with me and wear my mask. Pretend you are the boatman and take the young lady to the island. Then, my lord, kill the god.'

The man held out a neatly folded silk gungdae. 'This is your gungdae embroidered by the young lady. I've stepped away from the ritual for the moment under the pretext of giving you this and receiving payment. Now I ask that you pay the price you promised.'

Quickly, the warrior took the gungdae and proffered in turn a pouch of silver coins. The boatman accepted the money and shed his clothing. The boatman dressed himself in the warrior's clothing and hat, the warrior dressed himself in the boatman's clothing and mask, and in the dim light outside it was impossible to tell who was who. Finally, the boatman hid the bow and arrows in the boat and told the warrior that he need now only do as instructed by the others.

'All of this was planned by the young lady. If the villagers find out, she will not be able to escape death. So, once you finish your task, turn the boat around and flee far from this place as quickly as you can.'

At the boatman's words, the warrior asked in response, 'But you have aided us. How will you escape being questioned by your neighbours?'

'I will take the money you have given me and start a new life in a different village. This, of course, is what the young lady has arranged for me.'

The boatman finished saying his piece and quickly vanished.

The warrior was impressed. 'She is quite the clever maiden.'

On the shore, the ritual was reaching its peak. The sounds of drums, the stringed geum and gongs rang out. The boat floated upon the water, its sides encircled by lanterns of blue and red silk; its deck heaped with white paper flowers folded by the village's married women; its hull hiding the warrior's curved gakgung bow and arrows. The depths of the sea, with whatever was lurking within, reflected the light of the boat like a pitch-black mirror.

The warrior obeyed the villagers' instructions and helped the maiden onto the boat. Thankfully, no one recognised the warrior's identity. The maiden wore cotton clothing and a white conical hat, and her head was bowed. She seemed neither frightened nor shy. Without a breeze or sail to catch it, the boat moved by itself toward the island, as though dragged by the currents. While the boat sailed forth and the shapes and sounds of the people of the coastal village faded into the distance, the maiden lifted her head.

Startled, the warrior clenched the oar. The maiden was beautiful. Her face, raised into the black night sky and blocking the light of the moon, had never been sullied by despair or hope. She was like pure white fabric that had never been cut. Like a magnolia petal that had suddenly fallen onto an ebony plank in her room. Like a flurry of snowflakes swirling in the chill night sky that one could see from the central hall. Hers was a fleeting pureness and brightness that made the warrior's heart ache. Pierced by such a potent feeling that he had never felt before in his life, the warrior didn't know what to do. But it wasn't his first time feeling such a feeling. The warrior had loved the maiden after he was born and before that too. He'd loved the maiden through all the moments he could and couldn't remember.

Ever so slowly, the maiden removed the warrior's mask and gazed upon his bare face. Tears gathered in her eyes and she smiled.

'It really is you. My husband, whom I have seen in my dreams. I have been waiting my whole life for you, my lord. I have crossed over from an unimaginable death now into an unimaginable life.'

The warrior could see the maiden's days of being confined to her room as she waited for the sound of the warrior's footsteps. He could see the waxing and waning of her days, over and over, as she waited for the eternal night to end and for the sky to brighten. He then unfolded the gungdae the maiden had made for him and saw the embroidery that used time as thread and life as a needle, stitch after careful stitch.

For the first time, the warrior witnessed the maiden's rumoured embroidery skill. It was remarkable enough that not a single thread was out of place and the colours shimmered in harmony like mother-of-pearl; but, more than anything, the warrior was mesmerised by its subject matter. The dazzling gold dragon that looked like it would leap from the silk and let out a roar at any moment unmistakably resembled the warrior. Even though the dragon's face wasn't human, its eyes and expression appeared unusually human-like; without a doubt, it hinted at the warrior being the dragon. On the one hand, she had dared to give the warrior the divine form of a dragon which belonged to the king. But she couldn't be called insolent for that, nor could the innocence and sincerity of her design be disregarded, for the maiden had grown up entirely ignorant of history and symbolism. Not only that, but since her dragon had never been seen on any country's flag, any architectural motif or any garment, it was questionable whether it was a dragon at all. The maiden had seen the warrior and known for the first time what a dragon was. Only a warrior would be able to defeat the sea serpent and save the maiden; soon, this warrior was bound to become that noble, divine creature.

The horrible scarlet snake writhed in pain under the dragon's claws – that is, the warrior's feet – and seemed like it, too, would leap from the silk and beyond the deck of the boat, into the ocean.

The maiden carefully placed the bow into this gungdae and held it out respectfully to the warrior. Seeing her hands, the warrior knew, with a more powerful certainty than he'd ever experienced before any battle, that he would be victorious. Wrought of mulberry wood and two pieces of water buffalo horn, his precious bow had seen countless wars of conquest, generation after generation, and had passed through the bloodied hands of his ancestors; now, peacefully enveloped in the gungdae, it looked as though it had finally found its home after a long time wandering. It was impossible to tell whether the gungdae had been made for the bow or the bow had been made for the gungdae.

'This must be how it feels when a liquor that has been laboriously brewed fills my bottle, when a vase of plum blossoms will bloom only when it is placed in my room. A merchant has tamed a fine horse for me, so why would I not make it run? My lady, I will not let your devotion and labour go to waste. I will punish this wicked spirit and free you and your village from the bridle that binds you.'

Lazily, the boat touched the island and the warrior helped the maiden out. The shrine had become dilapidated with no one to look after it; submerged in darkness, it watched the pair silently as they moved about. The maiden seated herself neatly on the floor of the shrine and the warrior hid behind a pillar and waited with his bow. Not long after, a fierce wind began to blow, the waves began to roil, and a huge dark mass rose toward the shore.

The serpent looked exactly as the maiden had depicted it in her embroidery. Its body was like that of a huge snake, and so incredibly long that it could coil around the island five times and still have length left over. Its back was a dark red like the colour of old blood, and its stomach was yellowish like the colour of old bones left lying on a battlefield. Two eyes embedded on its wide, flat head glistened an intense yellow, like droplets of oil, as they stared at the maiden. They were like a tyrant's eyes, full of greed that would never be satisfied; yet they seemed also like the jaundiced eyes of a weak elderly person who was alive but not alive. Its scales were either jagged and uneven or completely missing, its fin was in tatters, and its flesh, rotting in places and spotted with barnacles and seaweed, gave off a nasty odour.

Nothing at all could be seen of the stern, majestic sea serpent that swam the blue waters far and wide and commanded schools of fish. Instead, it looked like a monster cursed to rot because it could never die. A hallucination from the deepest lightless depths of the ocean that someone who was drowning would see in their loneliest, most terrified moment, that bone-weary sailors would see over a typhoon.

The serpent coiled once around the shrine and raised its head to look down at the maiden. Even faced with a stench that made her nose run and its crimson tongue that darted back and forth as though ready to swallow her up at any moment, the maiden, who sat primly with her white clothing gathered around her, did not have one hair out of place; she only looked resolute. She believed unwaveringly that the warrior would slay the serpent and rescue her, so there was no reason to be afraid. Her commendable behaviour made the warrior's spirits rise and he nocked an arrow to his bow. As he pulled back the bowstring, reading the wind and estimating the distance, the bow seemed to wriggle as if it were alive and its tip gleamed gold. The arrow aimed itself at the sea serpent's eye and, because it knew where it was to fly, all the warrior had to do was simply let go.

When the arrow hit the very centre of the serpent's eye, the serpent let out a scream and twisted its body. A surge of icy seawater rose and crashed onto the roof of the shrine. The old shrine, which looked like it would fall apart, on the contrary stood tall even under the powerful force of the water. But the serpent flailed, letting out an unbearable sound like a ship's mast breaking. At last, the serpent perceived the intruder and turned, eyes blazing with rage and agony, toward the warrior. When the serpent spewed a fierce, grating screech and went to challenge the warrior, the warrior drew his bow and this time pierced the serpent's other eye with an arrow.

The serpent reared its head. Scales rained down from its body, dark venom gushed from its mouth and blood flowed from its arrow-pierced eyes. The warrior furrowed his brow at the sight that he could hardly stand to watch. The serpent blocked the maiden and looked back and forth between her and the warrior. Then, with one final, massive shudder, the serpent's head crashed to the ground and its body stiffened. It moved no more.

'A creature that should never have existed in this land was clinging to life and now it is finally dead. For that, we should be thankful,' the warrior said.

After he'd plucked out his arrows, the sea came to collect

the serpent's carcass and swallowed it back into the depths. Then all around them was quiet, as though nothing had transpired. The next morning, when the munyeo learned that the sea serpent was dead and shared the news, people would stand before the vast, cruel sea and lament that there was now no one to protect their sons and husbands.

The warrior helped the maiden back onto the boat. With not a single scratch upon her, the maiden's appearance was as pristine as ever. Because she didn't know the whereabouts of her parents and had no one else to turn to, she simply followed the warrior.

The warrior took the maiden's hand into his own. 'Till now, my hands have only held bows and arrows, my feet have only walked the path of battle and my heart has only served my king and country. But after I met you, I learned what it was to love and long for someone. I knew this to be a principle of nature that predates any law made by man,' he said tenderly. 'You are like a fresh pearl held by the sea for a hundred years; even uncrafted, you are brilliant on your own. I shudder to think of how you were almost torn to pieces by the teeth of a hungry ghoul that could not tell apart a pearl oyster from a sea snail. But, by the grace of the gods, you are before me now, unharmed, and I can hardly contain my joy. If you would be my wife, I will polish you until your true brightness shines. I will cherish you all my life. So, I beg you, remove that dreadful funeral shroud and clothe yourself in wedding attire. Be my beautiful bride.'

At the warrior's words, the maiden pressed her forehead to his feet in a deep bow. She who had never been able to cry, for fear of tainting her holy proposal, finally wept aloud for the first time in her life and, in that moment, she was pitiful, yet shining brightly.

'My joy today overshadows the unfortunate life I lived, with needle and thread as my only companions. I came here sold as an orphan and grew into a humble girl who knows nothing in the way of etiquette, but if my lord will have me as his wife, I will gladly serve you as my husband for the rest of my life.'

Upon the sea, with only the full moon as their witness, the warrior and the maiden exchanged marriage vows. After the boat arrived smoothly at the warrior's homeland, the couple married amidst the well wishes of many. The guests who attended their feast looked upon the bride and groom and declared them to be an irreproachable match made in heaven.

## 3.

The warrior and the maiden who were now a couple lived like a pair of lovebirds. Everyone knew that the husband cherished his wife dearly and that the wife was ever devoted to her husband. At first, the warrior's mother had been deeply worried. Because the maiden had been locked up according to her village's barbaric custom, not only did she know nothing about the law or about housekeeping, she was also like a ten-year-old girl who knew nothing about the ways of the world. What use would she be? But the maiden, who was sweet and bright, cared for her mother-in-law devotedly and learned everything from her in no time. She grew skilled in managing their farmland and supervising the slaves, faithfully held jesa rites for the dead, and gave birth to a healthy boy and raised him flawlessly. Then, at last, right before the warrior's mother died of an illness, she said she was pleased to have a wise daughter-in-law and gladly left her the keys to the storeroom.

Above all, there was no one in the neighbourhood who could match the maiden's gift for needlework. With the skill she had mastered over a lifetime, she added to the charm of her home and the beauty of her family. She embroidered auspicious gilsang patterns on her son's vest, thickened the lush bamboo grove that wrapped around the folding screen in her husband's quarters, and made a single lotus flower bloom becomingly on a norigae attached to her skirt. Whether it was a seat cushion, a quilt, cutlery sleeves or coverings for rice bowls, each had been made by her hand; every corner, seen and unseen, had such an exquisite, mysterious sort of elegance to it that those who lived there lived in luxury and those who visited couldn't help but marvel every time.

The more the warrior looked at his wife, the lovelier she became, until she seemed like a jewel itself in his embrace. When he was by her side, he felt at ease and forgot his cares; when he was separated from her, his heart was always steady and sure, so he was able to follow his orders as a soldier with loyalty. They had no trouble moving through life as a loving couple and, even as he grew older, whenever the warrior looked upon his wife the heavy scent of her powder made his heart race giddily, like he was a boy atop a donkey who'd encountered a bewitching ginyeo for the first time. Even though the warrior had never actually had his heart stolen by such a courtesan, nor did his wife look anything like one. Watching his wife's white forehead as she sat engrossed before her embroidery hoop, moving her needle, with a small frown creasing her brow, the warrior found her adorable and a small smile came unbidden to his lips. As it was his nature to be upstanding and intolerant of mistakes, whether his or someone else's, the warrior was a strict father who rarely saw fit to shower his gifted son with praise. Only in front of his wife did he become gentle, sometimes even turning into a silly, awkward little boy, so that the maidservants snickered under their breath and spoke ill of their calm mistress.

But that is not to say the warrior did not care deeply for his son. His son had a clear face and longish hands like his mother and dark brows and a stocky frame like his father. He was the image of his father when he used his slingshot to shoot birds, and his crafting skills were like his mother's when he whittled a toy knife out of firewood. The warrior showed him his gakgung bow and told him how to handle it carefully, as though he were speaking about a beast. When his son's eyes shone and his boyish hands felt up and down the bow, the warrior promised him, 'When you are grown and learn the ways of archery, I will pass on this bow to you.'

The warrior's family, whom everyone envied, encountered their first signs of discord when a royal decree arrived from the palace.

The king stated that, because noble families hoarded high-class silks and ornaments from foreign lands and tended to compete with one another to throw the most extravagant banquets and ceremonial functions, the discipline of the country was growing lax. Thus, the use of lavish silks and embroidered goods was banned henceforth. Moreover, the warrior's wife enjoyed gifting her embroidered norigae and incense pouches to other households, but the king frowned upon this, insinuating that she went around using them as bribes for advancing her husband's career. The warrior gravely summoned his wife and told her she was to show more restraint in her embroidery.

As always, his wife listened attentively to everything the warrior had to say before she spoke.

'This is unjust, my lord. It is nothing but slander spoken by those who are jealous of you. Do you not know that my gifts have no other motive than to give joy to those who are dear to me?'

'My wife, how could I not know this? But I cannot sit back and hear my family name be dishonoured, nor can I, as a soldier, disobey a strict order from the king. Indeed, because silks and embroidery are luxury goods, an excess of them becomes a weakness. My wife, your embroidery is precious by its very nature and those who receive it may want to repay you simply out of gratitude; I may have benefited from their favour without even my knowing.'

'My lord, I am not clever so I find it difficult to comprehend what you are saying. Before, you said my skill in needlework was my finest virtue as a woman and found my acts of generosity toward others commendable. I do not understand the reason why your words now are different from your words then. I still remember so vividly the joy on your face when I presented my gungdae to your bow. Are you not pleased to have such garments and household goods now blessing your home?'

His wife had only questioned him because she didn't understand. But even though she meant no harm, the warrior found her manner of speech to be disgraceful and felt his own innate stubbornness come to a boil. Even though inwardly he felt pity for her, he couldn't stop himself from being brusque.

'That spinning and sewing are considered meritorious deeds for a woman means that through making clothing, keeping the house clean and providing meals, she does precisely the tasks that are necessary for her family to live. It does not mean that she flaunts her skill and uses gold and silver thread to adorn fancy silks. Besides, I am not telling you to never embroider again. I am asking that you refrain from it unless it is something that is necessary, to show humility and be mindful when you handle your fabric and thread. I am asking you to be understanding, if you can, for it is better to give no gift at all than to give one that causes misunderstanding. You are no longer a maiden trapped in her room with nothing but embroidery to keep her company. You are the lady of this house. Your position now is different from what it was then – how can the same logic apply?'

The maiden was bewildered and disappointed by her husband's words, but when she thought about it carefully she came to understand and eventually agree that he was correct. So, she adhered to his guidelines. She changed her small pieces of art and decorations into plainer items and did not give gifts outside of certain joyous occasions. Even when she stitched garments for her husband and son, she abided by the king's ban and showed restraint in her use of fabrics and adornment.

The maiden continued to embroider as she had in the past, only now she made things for her own enjoyment rather than household items or garments to use in daily life. Because even if she made norigae or pouches, no place would take them; and even if she made belts and vests, no one would wear them; and even if she made pillow ornaments or coverings for bowls, no home would use them. Such craftsmanship should have been hung upon the walls of their home and admired like the embroidery paintings they were; but, wanting to faithfully follow her husband's orders, the maiden did not use her crafted goods even as decoration. They merely accumulated, untouched.

Now the maiden's embroidery was of no use to her family or her friends. It could not be on display regardless of whether it was made to delight someone or to repay them. It could not be dictated by nor dedicated to her husband's words. The maiden became forlorn, like she'd lost a dear love, but she could do nothing about it. Because she didn't want to be a woman who flaunted her skill in embroidery and desired to be world-famous, or a woman who decorated herself in gold and silver thread to rise above her humble birth and covet wealth; she needed to be a good wife to her husband and a good mother to her son. Because that was what she'd promised, long ago, when she was on a boat upon the quiet sea, under the light of the full moon. Because that was what she'd promised when she took the hand of her dear husband who had come to her from her dreams to rescue her.

Except, the maiden had the freedom to decide what to embroider upon her cloth. She sat where the sunlight was the brightest – in front of a window that showed her nothing but other houses and the mountain – and, with her embroidery hoop in hand, she let herself imagine. Landscapes with caves and valleys and volcanos. The North Star, continents and the paths of glaciers. With an ink stick she sketched all the images in her head and then used her colourful silk threads atop them to make stitch after careful stitch. Adding layer upon layer of shape and colour, the maiden's world came to life in her embroidery hoop. A world that once had been shuttered because of her husband's words, but was now wide open. A world that once couldn't be completed without her husband's word, but had now been finished.

When the maiden had made her embroidery painting ninety-nine blocks wide, the warrior experienced something strange.

The warrior dreamed that he was watching as thousands of supernatural dokkaebi fires speckled the western mountain with their radiance and surged down to the capital, howling. The fires swirled together to form a single huge blaze in the sky. They flickered and flared their way toward the warrior's land and descended to the earth. His vast rice paddies and fields became so completely consumed in flames that the whole world itself seemed to be burning bright. Yet in front of the fire, in white ceremonial attire, his wife was dancing for joy.

The warrior woke from his ominous dream in a cold sweat. He looked beside him. Bathed in the blue light of dawn streaming in from their window, his wife was sleeping peacefully. Seeing her smile crookedly like an infant fussing in its sleep, he dismissed the dream as a silly nightmare and tried to fall asleep once more.

The next morning, thunder cracked in the dry air and lightning struck and felled a thick tree beside the barley field, causing a fire to spread. The warrior and his wife rounded up the slaves to pour water on the flames but their efforts came up short and the fire spread out of control. Overnight, swathes of fertile land that had once been tended to by countless people turned into pitch-black charcoal.

At the time, the warrior was too preoccupied with handling the disaster to recall his dream from the previous night.

A few months later, he had another strange dream. This time he dreamed that a bird flew into his sleeping son's room. It was more of a bizarre-looking beast than a bird, with the head of a tiger, the beak of an eagle, the wings of a crow and the body of a serpent. The beast trotted to his son's pillow, cocked its head and let out a squawk. And then it pecked his son's neck with all its might and killed him. The door to the room swung open and his wife, dressed in white ceremonial attire, stepped inside, primly gathered up the beast and bade it fly out of the window. Here and there, droplets of blood dripped onto the ground.

The next day, the warrior had promised to take his son hunting in the forest with him for the first time. Thinking that his dream from the previous night had felt ominous, the warrior considered giving up, but he had delayed their outing on several occasions already and now his son was pestering him. Eventually, he decided that it was foolish to let a mere dream frighten him and headed to the hunting grounds with his son. He showed his son how to pursue the tracks of beasts living on the mountain, how to ready one's bow, and how to collect the carcass. After hunting rabbit and roe deer, they were happily thinking about heading back home when, suddenly, a huge boar appeared and began charging after father, son and their attendants. Amid the panic, the warrior's son fell off a cliff and perished instantly.

At the sight of her son's gruesome, mangled body, his wife wailed as though her own intestines had been cut out of her. The warrior, too, gave in to a profound feeling of sadness and guilt. He was mired in regret. That if only he had waited until his son was a little older, if only they had been a bit more careful in the woods, if only they had come home earlier, none of this would have happened. So when he heard people at the funeral whispering that because of her humble origins his wife had brought an unlucky energy with her, he lost his temper. This time he remembered his dream, but, seeing how his wife sobbed with grief before her son's body, he could not – nor did he even want to – associate her with the wife he'd seen in his dream. His wife must be pure. She must bear no cracks in either her mind or her body. She must be more beautiful and more virtuous than anyone else. He did not want to consider whether his wife was responsible for their repeated misfortunes, as his ghastly dream had seemed to indicate.

However, one day after the funeral had been held and

his son was buried on the western mountain, the warrior spotted his wife's face as she was doing embroidery and experienced a sudden shock. His wife had been lost to her grief and floating from place to place like a ghost, but now, seated in front of her embroidery hoop, strength returned to her body and her complexion took on colour. Her eyes, which had been vague and dim when looking at anyone or anything, sparkled when they alighted upon her silk. The slice of sunlight reflected on his wife's white forehead as she sat engrossed, moving her needle, with a small frown creasing her brow, was both beautiful and far away. Like a thrush that had flown into a household in mourning and, after merrily chirping without a care in the world, disappeared. The warrior thought it had been a long time since his wife had looked so beautiful. Or perhaps he was the one who had forgotten his wife's beauty for a long time. But now her beauty did not bring a smile to his face – it scared him. He could not understand her, nor could he touch her. Time seemed to flow for her alone, while he was frozen in place; or perhaps she was anchored to a specific time while he was the one afloat.

Curious about what his wife was so diligently embroidering, the warrior rummaged through the handiwork that had been stashed away in her chest. And he turned pale with shock. Made with ten different techniques and a hundred kinds of dyed threads, he saw fantastical colours and shades that he had never seen before. It was not only the skill on display that astonished him; the subject matter astonished him even more. The dance of countless dokkaebi fires speckling a mountain. A beast with the head of a tiger, the beak of an eagle, the wings of a crow and the body of a serpent. Every single thing the warrior had seen in his dreams was in the embroidery, to the point that he was uncertain whether his dreams had originated from the embroidery or if the embroidery had come from his dreams. That wasn't all. Starlight shining from the night sky in the Land of Bliss. The King of Hell, household gods, relics. Tears shed by evil spirits with horns and tails. All the things that occurred within a flower bud before a flower bloomed. Ants attending their queen through a huge palace maze. The lonely face of a prince banished to earth from heaven.

'This is vulgar beyond words. There is not one thing here that is proper or right; it is so full of that which is fantastical and wicked, I am ashamed even to look.'

The warrior took every single item his wife had ever embroidered and burned them in the furnace. Priceless decorative pieces, folding screens, norigae, pouches and quilts all went up in flames. A black smoke, along with its awful stench, rose up through the chimney and blanketed the sky. It took seven days for every stitch of embroidery to burn to a heap of ashes; seven days for the smell of burning to fade in the wind; seven days for all the smoke to be lifted and for the colour of the sky to be visible again. With everything gone, the house had become barren. It looked nothing like the house it used to be.

The warrior strictly forbade his wife from doing any more embroidery and threw away her hoop, needles and thread.

'Your embroidery is bringing ruin upon this family.'

Weeping, his wife said, 'You know well that embroidery was my only joy for so long. How could you be so heartless?'

His wife pleaded with him but the warrior had no mind to listen. Because he could not accept that embroidery had been his wife's only joy in life.

Although there were no further mishaps, his wife came to suffer a lingering illness and eventually became bedridden. She couldn't swallow her food properly, her body alternated between burning up like a fire and cooling down like a corpse, and when she spoke it was mostly nonsense that was hard to understand. The warrior summoned famous doctors to her side who burned cones of mugwort on her body and performed acupuncture, but her condition did not improve. He fed her every medicinal herb they recommended and made her drink healing water they said was precious, but still she did not get better. He stayed awake through the night beside her, spoke to her, offered her the teas and snacks she'd always loved, but still she did not get better. On sunny days, he took her in the palanquin to see an acrobatics show or a talchum performance. On the evenings of festival days, they went around the capital city and he took her to watch pungmul folk music and hear jokes; she would smile for a moment then, but become gloomy once more when they returned home. His wife only wanted to do embroidery. The only things she wanted to touch were her needles and thread. The only people she longed for were not her living husband nor her dead son, but the characters on her silk. The more his wife behaved like this, the angrier and more restless he became. The warrior believed embroidery was to blame for his wife's illness, and that for her to get better she needed to forget it completely.

As his wife's illness progressed, the house too began to fall apart. Dust gathered on the floors that she could not touch, the servants grew lazy and told lies, the seeds and vegetables in the storeroom rotted away, and outside, wild rumours swirled around the warrior's household. Things like she became sick because the warrior deemed her of lowly birth and abused her. Or she wasn't sick, she was locked away because she had taken a slave for a lover and was carrying his child. Whenever relatives visited, they offered words of advice. To try this medicine or find that munyeo, or even that the warrior should take a concubine. Finding all of this annoying, the warrior closed off his ears and eventually closed and locked his front gate too. He had simply wanted to be with his wife for longer. Everything he had said and done had only been to keep his wife by his side. Because he had lost his wealth and he had lost his son, and he did not want to lose his wife as well. But his wife was like pure white fabric that had never been cut, a magnolia petal that had suddenly fallen onto an ebony plank, a flurry of snowflakes falling from the night sky. And just as fleeting as had been her beauty, so fleetingly had she withered away, and that seemed like no process that could be stopped by man.

While they struggled through the winter, the maiden was unable to take a single step outside her room and only stared vacantly out her window to pass the time. As the ceaseless wailing of the northerly wind made its way into her room, the maiden didn't think about whether she wanted to die or not, she only thought she wanted to see the flowers bloom. Then, on one full-moon night on the threshold of spring, the maiden had a strange dream.

Someone was knocking at the front gate. When her husband donned his overcoat and stepped outside, he saw an older woman standing there modestly. She showed him a package wrapped in paper and said it was a medicine that would be good for the maiden's illness. Without hesitation, the maiden's husband let the woman inside.

In her delirium, the maiden heard the door to the room open and then close. When she opened her eyes, an older woman was standing in the middle of the room and staring at her with large, bright eyes. Without a word, the woman brought a hand to her own forehead and tore the skin from her face. Where the skin had been torn, there was not a woman's face but a man's. The maiden knew who this man was right away. The other day, when her husband had taken her to the marketplace to watch a talchum performance and acrobatics show, this man had been the clown who had balanced on a dizzyingly high tightrope with a fan in his hand.

'Why have you come here? I can no longer do embroidery. My illness is so far gone that no medicines can cure it. There is nothing you can do to help me, nor is there anything I can do to help you.'

The clown laughed heartily at the maiden's words.

'What use is your precious embroidery to a lowly wretch like me? And what ability does an idiot like me have that would cure your sickness?'

The clown's swarthy face bore a scar and his hands were rough. The lowly clown, who was yet free because of his lowliness, approached the maiden and stroked her cheek.

'Come away with me. I will show you the green meadows, the mountain peaks blanketed in snow, the golden fields of barley that ripple in the breeze. I will take you to the grand palaces and gardens, among the bustling crowd in the marketplace, into the heady fragrance of plum blossoms and water lilies and forsythias and peonies. I will introduce you to elephants and monkeys and black-skinned girls from foreign lands, to the mother and father who sold you. I will do this for you with my fan, my mask and my dance.'

As she listened to the clown speak, the maiden felt her body grow lighter and lighter. Her fever broke, her clouded eyes brightened and her breathing grew peaceful. She grasped the clown's extended hand, cleared off the remnants of her illness from the sickbed, and lightly got to her feet.

The clown unwrapped the paper parcel. It did not contain medicine, but a large fan. He unfurled the fan and fanned it once. A whirlwind rose inside the room. The maiden's navy-blue skirt that was finely embroidered with hydrangeas fluttered, and her small white hands spread open in the air. When the wind died down, the clown and the maiden had vanished without a trace; and, in the empty room, only a single hazy slice of sunlight shone.

## 4.

After his wife died, the warrior shut himself up in his house and met with no one. He had no intention to remarry. He drove out the servants, sold all of his farmland and his slaves, and used the money to drink and be alone. Passers-by would point out the warrior's home and click their tongues. Some said his past prosperity had all been in vain, others wondered how much he must have loved his wife to end up like this, but none of their words reached him.

Autumn leaves gathered in the well. Dandelion, chickweed and goosefoot grew in the garden and swayed in the wind. His neglected bow rotted away in a corner of the tea parlour. The warrior grew old and his wife grew vast. She was in every direction. Her face was in the sky and her breath passed through the air; her bone dust had been mixed and churned with the soil and her eyes had settled in the water. The warrior had loved the maiden after he was born and before that too. He'd loved the maiden through all the moments he could and couldn't remember. Compared to his love, the time the warrior had spent with his wife had been but a moment; the body of his wife held by him had been but one grain.

One morning, the warrior gathered his rotted bow, arrows and quiver, opened the front gate with its broken hinges and stepped outside. As he went down the road, looking as though he was about to fall flat on his face, everyone who encountered him thought he was crazy. But the warrior paid them no mind and kept walking and walking. He ran into a band of thieves and had his money stolen. He was chased by a tiger and had his leg gnawed off. Children threw stones at him until his flesh grew soft and rotten. He was soaked by the river and the rain. His clothes were turned to rags by sandstorms. Only then did the warrior arrive, at last, at the coastal village.

This time there was no need to request a gungdae to be made as an excuse to be there. No one prevented the warrior from entering the village. No one would have guessed the rotten tree branches he carried were his bow and arrows. Certainly no one would have guessed that this old man with dirty grey hair, a face covered in age spots and one leg missing had been the young man who killed their god and made away with their sacrifice all those years ago. Even if they did manage to recognise him, there was no reason to harass him.

It had been a long time since the sea serpent that was supposed to protect the village had died. The villagers were learning how to use their own two feet to stand up to the whims of nature and survive even without offering a sacrifice. Only the shrine, standing tall on the island, silently watched over the village.

The warrior searched the village for traces of his wife. He asked every person he encountered about the orphan who had been sold and brought here, the maiden who had been raised as a sacrifice to the god, the bride who had run away with a warrior. When and where had she been born? Whose daughter had she been, what had been her name? Some people said they didn't know. Some people said they didn't remember. Someone said she might've been the daughter of a woman who picked herbs at the foot of a mountain up north. Then someone beside that person shook their head and said she was the love child of a crazy woman from a farming village down south. Then someone opposite that person shook their head again and said she was the daughter of a couple who'd reigned over the slums in the capital; their bodies had been found the previous winter, the day the snow pellets fell, locked in an embrace. Their maiden only existed as the maiden to them, so her life before she was the maiden was imaginary, a rumour, an old story.

But the island would know.

The warrior stood on the beach and gazed at the island. It had seemed so far away when he'd rescued the maiden and sailed the boat. But it did not seem so far now; the shrine could be seen vividly from its spot on the clear horizon. Just as no one remembered when the island had come to exist, no one remembered when the shrine on the island had been built. Only that the shrine had been like part of the island's geology from the very beginning. Even if the village disappeared, the embroidery was set on fire and no records were left behind, the shrine would remain on the island. The warrior was not afraid that love would continue to exist at that shrine, even though the maiden he'd rescued, the serpent he'd fought and the confidence he'd had to grasp his bow had all vanished.

The warrior walked into the sea. The sea gently tugged at his clothing like a friendly innkeeper. But it was not just the sea. All the obstacles that had ever blocked his path disappeared. Even the resistance of the air and the water faded. Dyed in the colours of the setting sun, the warrior's white hair spilled into the water like paint. Copper scales sprouted from his body. The skin on his stomach became covered in ivory, his back grew a fin and his arms shrank smaller and smaller until they finally vanished. The sea serpent swam the blue waters far and wide, commanding schools of fish, and then descended into the deepest light-less depths of the ocean.

A few people who raced after the old man staggering into the sea witnessed this sight. Just off the coast, a few people who were drowning without anyone's knowledge, in their loneliest and most terrified moment, grabbed hold of the sea serpent's white fang. A few bone-weary sailors saw the sea serpent's brilliant amber eyes over a typhoon. The people who had the good fortune to make it back to their hometown would sit in front of a glass of liquor and recount the adventure and attest to its truth. On days the tempests made it impossible to take out the boats, the people would gather in small groups and speak of the legend of the warrior; of the outsider who walked into the sea; of the old man who lost his mind because he couldn't forget his dead wife, who then became the guardian god of the sea by the village. From time to time, the fishermen went to the island and left straw dolls in skirts along with alcohol and rice cakes on the shrine, and prayed for the safety of their boats and a good haul of fish for the year. At some point, their custom of leaving straw dolls changed into leaving live maidens.

This was how the village started its offering of maidens to the god.

# Author's Note

I've been preoccupied with stories about 'damsels in distress' for a long time. How I'd be able to save these damsels became a major point of interest, and as I set out to solve this problem, I failed again and again. I was the hero who always failed.

When I turned the records of my failures into a book, it felt like the damsel inside me had finally escaped her long period of distress.

Now, on to writing the next story.

June 2021
Amil

# About the Author

Amil is a South Korean writer and translator. She has won numerous awards for her short stories, including the SF Award in the Short-Mid Novel category for 'Roadkill' and the SF Award Grand Prize for 'Rabbi'. Amil has translated works by authors including James Baldwin, Joyce Carol Oates, Jeanette Winterson, R. O. Kwon and Lucas Rijneveld into Korean. *Roadkill* is her debut in English, with her novel, *The Forest Called You*, forthcoming in 2026.

# About the Translator

Archana Madhavan translates Korean poetry and prose into English. Her book-length works include Kim Hyun's *Glory Hole* (co-translation, 2022) and Amil's *Roadkill* (2025). Her translation of Lee Jenny's first book of poetry was short-listed for the Granum Translation Prize in 2023 and won the Malinda A. Markham Translation Prize in 2024. She lives in San Jose, California.